NEW
PEOPLE

■ ■ ■

N·E·W PEOPLE

DANZY SENNA

RIVERHEAD BOOKS

NEW YORK

2017

RIVERHEAD BOOKS
An imprint of Penguin Random House LLC
375 Hudson Street
New York, New York 10014

Copyright © 2017 by Danzy Senna
Penguin supports copyright. Copyright fuels creativity, encourages diverse
voices, promotes free speech, and creates a vibrant culture. Thank you for
buying an authorized edition of this book and for complying with copyright
laws by not reproducing, scanning, or distributing any part of it in any
form without permission. You are supporting writers and allowing Penguin
to continue to publish books for every reader.

Library of Congress Cataloging-in-Publication Data

Names: Senna, Danzy, author.
Title: New people / Danzy Senna.
Description: New York : Riverhead Books, 2017.
Identifiers: LCCN 2016045954 (print) | LCCN 2016054539 (ebook) |
ISBN 9781594487095 (hardcover) | ISBN 9780698172463 (ebook)
Classification: LCC PS3569.E618 N49 2017 (print) | LCC PS3569.E618
(ebook) | DDC 813/.54—dc23
LC record available at https://lccn.loc.gov/2016045954
p.   cm.

International edition ISBN 9780735219410

Printed in the United States of America
1   3   5   7   9   10   8   6   4   2

Book design by Lauren Kolm

FOR JOERITTA

Something got a hold of me, Oh yes it did.

—PEOPLES TEMPLE CHOIR, 1974

■ ■ ■

She wasn't expecting to see him here tonight. Now, her face feels warm as she watches him step onto the stage and pick up the microphone. He stands like a teenager, slouched and ambivalent, hands shoved in his pockets, as if he's been forced to appear, forced to read his poetry before strangers. Maria first met him several months ago—and now, it seems, he is everywhere she looks. Or maybe she is everywhere he looks. Just last week she ran into him at a restaurant. He was there—sitting at the bar alone, drinking a beer—when she arrived to meet a friend. She stopped to say hello and he said a polite hello back, frowning as if he couldn't remember her name. Afterward, she sat only half listening to her friend rattle on about work, conscious with every breath of his form at the bar.

In the audience, listening to his voice, she realizes that she has been waiting to see him again. She feels uneasy with this awareness. She keeps her eyes fixed on his sneakers, which are dirty and giant. It is too much to look at his face.

Her fiancé, Khalil, sits beside her. Khalil's sister, Lisa, sits on the other side. They flank her. The audience around her, who moments before were laughing and hooting at the last performer, a girl who swung her long hair from side to side, seems to have gone unusually still, alert, as if at the precipice of some new awareness.

Khalil places a hand on Maria's knee and leans in and whispers, This guy's pretty good. She nods, glancing away from the stage toward the back of the club. It is raining outside. Maria thinks she should tell Khalil she feels sick and wants to go home—because in a way, this is true. But she doesn't. She stays seated, her face turned away toward the exit, and when it's all over, she follows Khalil and Lisa to the front of the club; they both want to say hello. She hangs back, listening to them speak. Lisa is saying something about a line she likes from his penultimate poem. That's the word she uses. *Penultimate.* Khalil is smiling, nodding in agreement.

The poet looks embarrassed by their praise. He keeps scratching his arm as he stares at the floor.

Maria hovers in the background, her fists clenched in her pockets.

The poet's eyes discover her.

You good? he says.

She nods, chokes out the lie: I'm good.

■ ■ ■

In her dream that night she is sitting on a blue velvet sofa, reading the pages of a friend's novel. She realizes in the dream that it is a perfect story she is reading. She is miserable that she did not write it. She knows she will never write a book like this. She will never write a work of fiction. She is a scholar; she only works with given materials.

She wakes up hot with envy. She has to remind herself that the novel doesn't exist outside of her dream, nor does the friend who wrote it.

Khalil is asleep beside her. There is a ticking sound coming from the kitchen. Maria closes her eyes, thinking of the poet. She remembers his face and the way he stood half-turned away from the audience. She remembers, with photographic clarity, the slope of his forehead and the small scar cutting through his eyebrow. Warmth and a kind of preemptive grief move through her body.

Khalil looks politely bored in his sleep, as if he's listening to somebody recounting a dream.

Maria is twenty-seven. She is engaged to marry Khalil, who loves her unequivocally. She is the one he has been waiting for his whole life. Maria loves Khalil. She never doubts this. He is the one she needs, the one who can repair her.

They met in college on the other coast years ago, so they have, in a sense, grown up together. It is sometimes hard for Maria to see where one of them ends and the other begins. Their favorite song is Al Green's "Simply Beautiful." Their favorite movies are *Sammy and Rosie Get Laid*, *Chameleon Street*, and *Nothin' But a Man*. Their favorite novel is *Giovanni's Room*. Khalil says they make each other complete. Their skin is the same shade of beige. Together, they look like the end of a story.

They live together in Brooklyn in a neighborhood that is changing. It is November, 1996. Interspersed among the old guard—the Jamaican ladies with their folding chairs, the churchy men in their brown polyester suits—are the ones who have just arrived. It is subtle, this shift, almost imperceptible. When Maria blurs her eyes right it doesn't appear to be happening. They dance together at house parties in the dark. *If I ruled the world*, they sing, their voices rising as one, *imagine that. I'd free all my sons*.

Maria is writing a dissertation. She has been granted a small fellowship to live on in this final year, so she can focus on completion; it isn't enough to foot their bills, but Khalil carries the rest. Khalil works in computers. He makes enough as a part-time technology consultant to support them both. His real passion is the business he and a friend from college are trying to get off the ground. Khalil has explained their plan to Maria—it will be an online community of like-minded souls, modern tribalism at its best. He says it will make them rich someday. He is looking for investors.

Maria spends her days at the social science library on 118th and Amsterdam, poring over materials from a long-gone time and place. It is already late fall and she has come to rely on rituals to get her work done. She wears the same peacoat and the same red gauzy scarf. She stops at the same deli and orders the same thing from the burly guy behind the counter, a buttered bialy and a coffee, light and sweet. She keeps the same assortment of snacks in her purse: a bag of salted cashews, a chocolate bar, a bottle of water.

There is a window beside her carrel where she sometimes pauses to watch the cold air sharpening the edges of buildings. She has decided all university campuses are alike—the sense of possibility and stasis. She thinks this too: all graduate students, if you look closely enough, exude the same aura of privilege and poverty.

The photo on Maria's university ID is now four years old. It was taken the year she and Khalil moved here from California. In the picture she looks like a different Maria. It isn't just the golden brown of her skin, and it isn't just her bangs, which hang long over her eyes. It is her smile, crooked and loose, and the expression in her eyes, some barely contained hilarity. She looks preserved in the moment before you burst into laughter. She can no longer remember what was so funny.

Maria's subject is Jonestown, the Peoples Temple. She entered the program planning to study seventies-era intentional communities—the bonds of kinship forged among unrelated people. Once she started investigating Jonestown, she could not look away.

She knew then only the most basic facts, the ones that had become part of the detritus of the culture: That Jonestown was a cult. That the group's leader, Jim Jones, wore sunglasses everywhere. That he and his followers committed mass suicide together one day in the jungles of South America by drinking the Kool-Aid.

The question that guided her then was the most banal, the one posed by all holocausts: How does such a thing happen? She was guided by a line from Juvenal's *Satires: Nobody becomes depraved overnight.*

Now, so many years into it, her focus has shifted. She wants to know not how they died but how they kept themselves going. There is no memorial to the people of Jonestown. The remote jungle in Guyana that they cleared, where they built a society, has long been reclaimed by vegetation. The last visitor to the site reported finding only the

barest remnants of what once was: a tractor engine, a rust-
ing file cabinet, the metal drum they had used to poison the
liquid before they drank it.

The music they made—the tapes they recorded—are all
that is left of the people who lived there. They sang in the
early days in Indiana where the church began. They sang
while they rode the fleet of Greyhound buses from Indianapolis to Ukiah, California. They sang when they arrived
in Guyana, while they cleared the cassava and palm trees
with machetes. They sang while they cooked the rice and
oily gravy that was their main diet. They sang while they
cared for the children in the Cuffy Nursery. They sang in
the beginning and they sang at the end. It is all on tape.

Maria is trying to write about their music—an ethnomusicology of the Peoples Temple. She is trying to uncover
the modes of resistance in the hymns and melodies they recorded when they were alive. She is trying to excavate,
using their music, the clues not to why they would commit
suicide but to how they survived as long as they did. She
argued in her proposal that the music was a form of resistance to Jim Jones himself. Her project is going to be—is
supposed to be—a radical reclamation of Jonestown on be-
half of the people who built it.

The last time Maria saw her dissertation advisor, he was
packing up his office to go on sabbatical. He told her he
didn't think she'd found it yet, the true meaning of her

work. He said, You're still circling the jungle, Maria. You're still afraid to land.

When they said goodbye at the door to his office, he asked her if she was dreaming about Jonestown yet. Did it come to her at night?

She told him no, she wasn't dreaming of it yet. He smiled and said, Then you're not working hard enough. They need to be in your dreams.

Maria shows up every day. And every day she comes upon a new revelation about the people of Jonestown. Just the other day she discovered that the hand-painted sign they kept hanging in their pavilion, the one that read, *Those who do not remember the past are condemned to repeat it*, was a slight misquote of a line from George Santayana; the real quote said those who "cannot" remember the past. It seems to her this was a serious error, but she can't figure out why.

Today she closes her eyes and listens to an audiocassette of the Peoples Temple Choir album. It was released in 1973 when they were still based in the church front on Geary Boulevard in San Francisco. A copy of the actual LP is wrapped in plastic in the special collections library across campus. She has held it in her hands. On the cover is a photograph, a hundred choir members standing at the edge of a lake. The women are wearing floor-length blue satin gowns and the men are wearing starched white shirts. They look somehow both old-timey and hip, just like the music they make, which sounds a little bit gospel, a little bit rock and roll. The first cut is the children's song. They sound so clear and bright that she feels as if they are here with her. Their voices rise and fall with what she imagines is the conductor's baton.

> *He keeps me singing a happy song.*
> *He keeps me singing it all day long.*
> *Although my days may be drear,*
> *He always is near,*
> *And that's why my heart is always filled with song.*

■ ■ ■

The next time she sees the poet, she is walking through the Village, going to meet Khalil for lunch with friends. It's a cold afternoon. The weather has turned. She has just come from the library. She is wearing her peacoat and her red scarf.

She sees him before he sees her. He's standing up ahead looking in the window of a record shop. She catches her breath and stops several feet away.

The restaurant where she's headed is up around the block and she is already a few minutes late, but instead of going on her way she just stands there stiffly until the poet looks up and sees her.

He does a double take, squints at her, as if trying to remember how he knows her. Then he smiles slightly and walks toward her. Hey, you, he says.

She says his name aloud, thinking, not for the first time, that he doesn't remember hers. They've met several times in loud places, and they've shaken hands, but she cannot recall him ever once saying her name. She is too embarrassed to tell it to him now.

Where you headed?

Meeting a friend. She looks away, toward the street, the omission burning on her tongue.

You live around here?

She tells him she lives in Brooklyn.

He makes a face. Do you like it there?

Then, before she can answer, he says: I hate Brooklyn. I never go there if I can help it.

She feels stung, as if he has just admitted to hating her. She wants to tell him Brooklyn was Khalil's idea, that he got it in his head long ago, before they left California, before they talked all senior year about wanting to join the Brooklyn Renaissance. But she doesn't say it.

There is a long, full silence. He is watching her. She feels his gaze as a physical thing, a heat moving across her skin. When his eyes move away her skin feels cold again.

Hey, you're friends with Lisa and Khalil, right?

She nods.

Right. I remember you.

She pauses. I'm going to meet them.

Don't let me keep you, he says, stepping aside to let her pass.

He is already looking beyond her at something in the distance, and she feels the cold again. She thinks maybe she's coming down with something.

She starts forward, but stops and turns back.

Do you even know my name? she asks.

He scratches his cheek, shrugs. Looks a little caught.

Maybe, he says.

It's Maria. I wasn't sure—because you never say it.

His eyes are amused. Maria, he says. Maria. Maria. Maria.

She laughs, tilts her face down, and walks away, her heart galloping. At the end of the block she glances back to see him still standing in front of the record shop. He is watching her, but he turns away when she spots him looking.

∎ ∎ ∎

Khalil and Lisa are already there, at a table at the back with three other people. Khalil is wearing his faded X T-shirt from college. His dreadlocks have long since passed the Basquiat stage but have not quite arrived at Marley.

Lisa is wearing a head wrap of brightly colored fabric, magenta and blue. She says, Maria, as always on CP time.

What took you so long? Khalil says, leaning forward to kiss her. He puts a hand on the small of her back.

A woman at the table, someone she knows, grabs Maria's hand and yanks it toward her.

Okay, I've got to see it. This is the famous ring. Oh damn, now this isn't fair.

It's a family ring, Khalil says. We had it restored, resized.

When he says "we" he means Lisa. She was in on this.

Lisa is younger than Khalil by two years. She goes everywhere with him. They don't look much alike. Lisa is darker than Khalil; she takes after their mother. Khalil takes after their father. Khalil is the firstborn, the beloved messiah. Lisa, in second-child tradition, has always been the more difficult one. Khalil once told Maria that his whole childhood was spent watching Lisa be carried out of restaurants, shrieking.

Some facts about Lisa: She has only ever dated white boys. She speaks fluent Italian. She has a framed poster for Fellini's *La Dolce Vita* on the wall of her apartment. She likes to read film theory in bed. It's still not clear what Lisa is going to do with all of her education, how she will build on all the years of good parenting that have gone into her. She was studying to be a pastry chef when Maria first met her; now she works in a French bakery in Soho, but everyone in the family knows it's temporary.

Lisa has discovered only since Maria became a part of their family that her darkness is something she can lord over people—that it is something superior to her brother's high yellow. Maria was surprised nobody ever told her this before. Lisa is beginning to understand that the very things she hated growing up, her kink and her color, have begun to have currency if you know where to go, who to be around, who to avoid, how to frame the conversation.

Lisa mentions her darkness a lot these days, how much darker she is than her brother and Maria—though really she isn't very dark unless she stands beside them. Maria didn't like Lisa the first time they met. She thought the head wrap made her look like she was either hiding something or trying to appear like an African objet d'art to the willowy white boy she was dating at the time. Maria thought Lisa was the kind of black person she would have avoided in high school. So was Khalil, for that matter. What was it they called those kinds of black people back in the day? Miscellaneous.

Now Khalil and Lisa are changing, turning into something closer to Maria, and she feels like Charon, leading them across the river to the dark side.

Lisa bought a T-shirt on the street in Harlem a few weeks ago that reads, *It's a black thing, you wouldn't understand.*

Maria sometimes catches sight of herself walking with them through the city and thinks what an unlikely arbiter of blackness she is. How strange that it should be she to ferry them across.

Here in the restaurant, the woman examines Maria's hand, twisting it this way and that, and Maria too peers at her own hand, the ring, as if it belongs to somebody else.

The stone glimmers as she tilts it beneath the light at different angles.

It is a large sapphire surrounded by twelve white diamonds. It belongs—belonged—to Khalil's grandmother, the one with the camp numbers tattooed on her arm. She lives on the Upper East Side. She has given her blessing.

Now that Maria is here, the conversation turns to the wedding. It always turns to the wedding.

She listens to Khalil and Lisa imparting the details as if it's they who are getting married. It will be at the lighthouse on Martha's Vineyard. It will be in May. They will break a glass (Jewish) and jump the broom (black).

Who's going to be there? the woman wants to know.

It is Lisa who answers. All the Niggerati.

* * *

That weekend, a filmmaker arrives at their apartment to interview them for a documentary about "new people." That is actually the working title of her film: *New People.* Her name is Elsa. She has frizzy blond hair and golden brown skin and green eyes. She stands in the foyer, glittering with snowdrops. In her strong teeth Maria can see the Scandinavian half of her heritage. She introduces the others she has brought with her—an Asian-American cameraman named Ansel with hair down to his waist, and a white woman with a buzz cut named Heidi. They crowd in the hallway, damp and smiling.

Elsa is older than Maria and Khalil. She is well into her forties. Maria does the math. This means she would have been born in the 1950s, the Era of Mulatto Martyrs—which Maria knows from the history books was a whole other scene. Maria and Khalil were each born in 1970, the beginning of the Common Era.

Elsa says that when she met Khalil at a party uptown, she knew he was perfect for the film. He wanted Maria to meet Elsa before they committed themselves to it. Khalil and Maria sit on the couch now while Elsa's crew hovers in the background, filming their conversation. Elsa wants them to talk naturally, to be spontaneous.

They tell jokes and share stories they have told before, stories that already feel like lore. His parents met at Freedom Summer and Maria's mother was once a member of SNCC.

Khalil says: Sometimes she teases me about acting Jewish. You know, like my rabbinical hand gestures. Sometimes I tease her about acting WASPy. The way she says "duvet" instead of comforter. We're like a Woody Allen movie, with melanin.

Elsa scribbles notes. After the interview she and her crew film Maria and Khalil walking hand in hand through Prospect Park. It is only late afternoon, the snow has melted, and it is nearly dark. The longer Elsa films, the more Maria and Khalil have to pretend they're having a conversation. Her mind is elsewhere. She is tired of being on camera already. She wants to be back in the library under the artificial lights with her papers spread out around her, the headphones playing the children's voices, a mystery about to be solved.

But back at the apartment, Elsa and her crew stick around. They film Maria and Khalil chopping vegetables in their kitchenette, making a Moroccan tagine while Ornette Coleman plays on the stereo. Afterward, they each sign forms agreeing to be in the movie. Khalil seems happy about it and Elsa, grinning, tells them how thrilled she is to have them on board. She says they are exactly the subjects she has been looking for. Maria goes through the motions, smiles along, but she is aware of a pain in her chest, a tightness to her breathing.

■ ■ ■

The apartment feels different after the crew has packed up and gone—more barren than it did before. Maria sits in bed, flipping through the brochure for Jonestown. She can see Khalil through the open door. He is seated in the living room, bare-chested in boxers, staring at something on the computer screen.

Maria brought the brochure home from the library the

other day. The girl on the cover is not somebody Maria recognizes from any of the other pictures she has seen of the collective. The girl is maybe fifteen years old and stands in the jungle, smiling, cradling a tiny sloth in her arms. The creature stares into the camera with sad humanoid eyes. Over the picture are the words *A feeling of freedom*.

Inside is a montage of photographs advertising the compound. The Peoples Temple Agricultural Project in Guyana was only two years old. After the earliest arrivals had spent months clearing the remote jungle outpost with machetes and tractors at Jim Jones's behest, hundreds of Americans—members of the San Francisco Church—relocated there. They lived together in the simple wooden cottages together, among the macaws, harvesting their own food. They even had a mascot, a chimpanzee named Mr. Muggs whose cage was next to Jones's own cottage.

Maria has stared at this brochure many times. She knows it was used to recruit new members from up and down the California coast. In the picture she stares at now, an old man stands beside an orange grove over the caption *Everything grows well in Jonestown, especially the children*. Below him is another image showing a smiling blond boy of ten or eleven holding two plump brown babies on his lap. On the next page, two women in kerchiefs sit on the ground of a nursery, tending to a row of toddlers who lie side by side in cots. The testimonials from those who have arrived sound ecstatic.

People are so free here and they look so different . . .
This is a new world—clean, fresh, pure—
Man, the Fillmore has seen the last of me!

The brochure goes on for sixteen pages. On the final page is a picture of a young man with his hair in neat cornrows, standing with his arm around a young woman, her hair in a wide Afro. Maria recognizes their faces. She knows they are siblings. She knows their names. Ronnie and Shanda James. She knows the exact brutal details of how their story will end. But in the picture she stares at now, it is still just the beginning.

■ ■ ■

I t is an active thing, this remembering him. Like rubbing a prayer bead in your pocket. She conjures him up in odd moments and it never fails to bring her a wave of pleasure. The thought of him makes her not so much relax as it seems to transport her, electrified, to a secret, happy place. She doesn't have much to draw upon—the conversation they had on the street where he repeated her name aloud, and before that, the fleeting moment when he glanced up at her in the club and asked if she was good. The light in the scenes that play in her mind is grainy and muted, like clips from an old movie, one of the films her mother used to love, maybe *Klute*. She imagines them together inside one of those movies, where the women had real faces and drooping, small breasts and the men were dirty and sly.

Now, as the subway train rumbles to a stop, she is jarred back to the present. She is in midtown. She pushes her way through the crush of dank, unmoving bodies. They don't bother to step aside. She barely makes it out before the doors close.

It is a weekday morning, but she is not headed to the library today. She is taking a day off from her work to go meet Khalil's grandmother, the one he and Lisa call Oma. Maria is going to try on wedding dresses in front of her and Lisa at the bridal salon on the fourth floor of Bergdorf Goodman. Lisa organized the excursion and made the appointment for them there with a bridal specialist. Lisa has arranged to pick up Oma at her apartment on the Upper East Side and bring her by cab to Bergdorf's.

Maria would have preferred to go somewhere cheaper, smaller—a thrift shop, perhaps—for her dress. But Oma wants to see her try on dresses at Bergdorf's. Oma is the bestower of the ring on Maria's finger and she cannot shake the sense that the ring will always belong to Khalil's family.

Khalil's parents live in Seattle, where he grew up. His father, Sam, grew up in New York City but went west after college. He is an epidemiologist specializing in global health initiatives. Khalil's mother, Diane, is a local television producer in Seattle. The Mirskys spent the bulk of Lisa's and

Khalil's childhood traveling the world. They are as tight-knit a family as Maria has ever known. Their homeland is one another. They seem most happy when they are together, sprawled around their brightly colored living room. They even have their own family whistle—a shrill birdcall they made up long ago to locate one another in foreign crowds when one got separated from the group.

Whenever Maria and Khalil go to visit them in Seattle, Diane prepares fresh fruit for their breakfast. She cuts it up and leaves it all laid out on a platter for them to start their day. Sam has a subscription to *Consumer Reports* magazine.

The Mirskys remind Maria of something her mother, Gloria, once said on the Fourth of July, standing on the balcony of her graduate student housing, her plastic cup of white wine held up to toast the fireworks that exploded over the Charles River. You got a few things right, America, she said. Jews and jazz. Happy birthday.

Gloria is dead now. She was diagnosed with breast cancer during Maria's final year of college. She died eight weeks later at a hospice called Transitions. She was forty-nine. She died with no survivors but her adopted daughter, Maria, and fifty thousand dollars in student debt. There was not a single piece of furniture or jewelry worth selling.

As Maria moves past the shops and peddlers and break-dancers in the station and toward the escalator, she hears somebody calling her name. The voice is warbling, female, unfamiliar. She stops and looks over the heads of strangers until she spots a young woman smiling and waving at her.

Maria. Maria. Maria.

She is jogging toward Maria beneath the flickering fluorescent lights of the station. She looks Maria's age and wears a blue business suit. The jacket has large shoulder pads and looks a decade out of style. Maria watches, puzzled, as the girl comes toward her, laughing, a little out of breath. Her dirty blond hair hangs in thin strands around her face, but her skin is clear and bright, her features fresh, like a girl in an acne cream commercial. She touches Maria's arm, leans in for a hug. She smells of a cheap floral drugstore perfume. Maria accepts the hug stiffly, struggling to remember where and how they met.

I saw you all the way downstairs but you didn't hear me. Wow. Wow. I can't believe it's actually you.

Maria searches the girl's face. She has slightly buck teeth, pale blue eyes, a smattering of freckles on her nose. She looks a bit like the eldest sister on *Eight Is Enough*.

Come on, she says. You remember me, don't you?

I'm sorry, Maria says. I'm drawing a total blank.

Okay. I'll give you a hint. College? Self-Defense for Women?

Maria remembers the class. How could she forget? There was a book that came out that year called *All I Really Need to Know I Learned in Kindergarten*. Maria has thought in the years since that she should write a book

called *All I Really Need to Know I Learned in College.*
More specifically, in Self-Defense for Women. That class
was where she learned to shout "NO!" from her diaphragm.
That was where she learned how to push away a man with
a butterfly motion of her arms, how to ram her knee into a
man's balls, how to stomp her heel onto his foot so that the
metatarsal bone would break, how to thrust her palm upward into his nose so that his nasal bone would go straight
through his brain, how to gouge out his eyes. Scoop into
them just right. That was where she learned how to "maxi-
mize the damage."

She remembers everything about that class—but she
doesn't recognize this girl standing before her.

We were partners, the girl says, blinking, looking a little
hurt. I'm Nora Convey.

The name. Of course. It sends her back. Nora Convey.
Sad-sack Nora Convey. Yes, they were partners all right.
But she doesn't look at all like the same person. Nora Convey. Distantly, she can see the old Nora, can make out the
faintest resemblance. But Nora has changed. She used to be
extremely overweight with acne. Now she is slim with this
clear, bright complexion. And something else is different,
something Maria can't put her finger on.

Remember? Nora says, grinning, nodding. Her teeth are
still slightly yellow. Some things never change.

Of course I remember you. Of course. I'm so sorry I
didn't see it.

No worries. You don't have to pretend. You won't hurt my feelings. Nobody recognizes me anymore. I don't blame them. I was . . . Nora crinkles her nose. You know. A different person.

Maria is unsure how to respond. She feels awkward. She remembers being disappointed whenever she was chosen to be Nora's partner. Once she'd had to stand inside the circle of other girls wearing a giant helmet and overalls with padding between her legs and attempt a "model mugging" on Nora. She remembers how weak Nora had been, how easy she had been to throw onto the mat. How irritated Maria had been that Nora didn't even really struggle. She'd had the thought at the time that Nora was a born victim.

And in a way, it seemed like the truth. Nora told the class one day about being bullied as a child. She described a particularly horrible bus ride home, where she'd sat in a kind of numb trance while the other kids threw candy wrappers and garbage at her.

The women in the self-defense class assured Nora she was a survivor. And maybe they were right after all, because she stands before Maria looking like an entirely different person.

The air in the station is sweet and thick; nearby is the grating manic tune of Michael Jackson's "Thriller." A crowd has encircled a dancer just a few feet away. Maria sees it is a child, an androgynous, raceless child moonwalking in the center, his or her hat tilted forward over his or her face, one white-gloved hand limp, snapping a beat as he or she moves backward on an invisible conveyor belt.

Nora turns to watch the child with Maria for a moment, both of them transfixed.

You were always so kind to me, Nora says. I mean, when you didn't have to be, you were kind to me. It's funny how you don't forget that sort of thing.

Maria tries to remember being kind to Nora. She can't think of one instance. She wasn't mean to her, but she wasn't kind either.

That was the semester she and Claudette had gotten high one night and written the worst protest poem in the history of the world together. Claudette and Maria did everything together that year. Claudette was a self-declared dyke—a black military brat who had come out of the closet upon her arrival at Stanford and shaved off her long "colonized" hair. No more Revlon three-minute relaxers. No more squeezing her bunions into anything but combat boots. No more fucking around.

Claudette was Maria's closest friend for a long time, before she wasn't.

That night, she and Claudette wrote a parody in Maria's dorm room of an epic poem called "Her Story." They scribbled it together, cackling hysterically on Maria's bed, then typed it up and printed it out and signed it Anonymous and at three in the morning walked through the cool night air to the offices of the school's feminist magazine. The poem, as she remembers it, involved the liberal use of the terms *my cunt-ry* and *Amerikkka*. It was a voice screaming from history's dustbin. They left it in the submissions box, then forgot about it and drove to San Francisco in Maria's ancient blue Volkswagen for a night of clubbing.

A few weeks later Maria was surprised to see their words published on the front cover of the feminist magazine. It had been distributed all across campus.

Nora is talking fast beside her. She is saying that she wants to find out what Maria has been up to all these years. She wants to tell her about her own amazing journey.

Maria is curious—as much about how Nora went from sad to happy as she is about what, exactly, Nora remembers of Maria's kindness. She wants to know the details of it. She glimpses a clock on a distant station wall. She still has twenty minutes before she's supposed to meet Lisa and Oma at the bridal salon. She tells Nora she has a few minutes to spare. She can walk with her at least.

Outside of the station, the sky is darker than it was when she left Brooklyn. It hovers, low, as if threatening to rain. The city seems all lit up for Christmas already, colors blinking and biting at the pedestrians who rush past.

Nora talks as they walk—tells Maria how she tried everything for years: pills, diets, therapy, even living on a Native American reservation for a year and taking peyote and enduring sweat lodges. She says she was trying to get free of the self-loathing inside of her.

People say children are resilient, Nora says, but it's not true. If kids were so resilient, why would we have a world of broken people out there? Why would we have so many people paying to talk to strangers? Childhood is a series of traumas that build up and make you forget who you really are. You know what I mean, Maria? So you have to find a way—a path—back to the person you were before it got so muddy.

Maria listens, trying to understand what Nora is saying. She keeps searching her face, trying to see the other girl, the fat girl, but the more she looks at this new face, the more she can't really remember what the other one, the old Nora, looked like. Not really. Just that she was overweight and felt so soft and clammy and weak in her arms when she model-mugged her in class.

Nora's words have an opaque quality to them.

Maria, she says, you were one of those rare popular girls who was also nice. I remember when you told me I was beautiful, Maria. That comment kept me going for years. Did you know that?

Maria doesn't remember being popular. She also doesn't remember telling Nora Convey she was beautiful. She is pleased by the description of herself nonetheless and feels a sort of swelling pride in her chest. When she catches sight of her own reflection in a store window, she sees she's smiling and there is a sort of excited gleam in her own eyes.

My mother always used to say that character is character, Nora says. Maria, you were always a good person. I always felt that about you, from the moment we met.

Nora stops walking and turns to face her. Maria wonders briefly if Nora is making a mistake, confusing her with somebody else. She says it aloud. Are you sure you're thinking of me? I'm not a bad person, Maria says, but I'm—

Of course I'm not confusing you with somebody else! Nora clucks her teeth. There's only one Maria Pierce. Gosh, Maria. Who would I be confusing you with?

Maria laughs a little, relieved. She stares at her reflection in the dark window behind Nora. Wait, was it after class? How did I say it exactly? Like, "You're beautiful." Just like that?

Hail begins to fall in pellets all around them. A sound of drumbeat on the glass. Nora squeals, laughing, and grabs Maria's arm. She pulls Maria inside the doorway of the building beside them. Maria shakes the ice off her jacket and looks around to see they are standing inside what looks like a hotel conference room.

There are people milling around, smiling, busy. She is surprised to see some of them smiling in their direction, waving, and then it dawns on her that they already know Nora. That this is where Nora was leading her.

Wait, she says. What is this place?

I'm about to show you.

There is a large sculptural display of books on a table nearby. All the books have similar covers. She squints and sees that they are all written by L. Ron Hubbard.

Nora is still talking. This is the place that saved my life. Do you know that I would have died had I not met my teacher one day just walking down the street? Truly. I would have died had she not led me through these doors, the way I've just led you.

An Indian-looking man and a black woman are waving at them from behind the stack of books. Maria offers a limp wave back. She sees Asian people, white people, Latino people, and black people moving around, working together in clusters, heading off together arm in arm to other parts of the building. When she was just a kid, Gloria told her never to trust a group of happy, smiling multiracial people. Never trust races when they get along, she said. If you see different races of people just standing around, smiling at one another, run for the hills, kid. Take cover. They'll break your heart.

Nora is standing too close to Maria.

Listen, I sense you're going through some difficult times, Maria. I can feel it coming off you. I'd like to administer a simple test that I think will help you. No strings attached. I just want to help you the way you once helped me.

Maria stares at her. Some small part of her thinks maybe the girl Nora is describing from college was a real person. She follows Nora into another room, still trying to remember telling Nora she was beautiful.

Nora invites her to take a seat at a table. There is a contraption on the table. She hands Maria a set of metal cylinders and then begins to fiddle with the machine. Maria dimly thinks of the poet, wonders what he's doing at the moment, if he's writing a poem alone in his apartment. She tries to imagine his apartment, what it smells like. It's automatic: She feels the rush of pleasure that his image conjures inside of her, doesn't even care that much that Nora is strapping something onto her arm. Thinking about him, she doesn't even care if she was ever kind or popular or if she ever really did tell Nora she was beautiful.

Nora fiddles with some dials until lights go on, then she begins to ask Maria questions.

Maria tries to answer as truthfully as she can.

What would you do if you saw a woman beating a child by the side of the road?

I don't know. What did the kid do?

Would you ever lie to save a friend's life?

Of course.

What would you do if you saw a dollar lying on the subway platform?

Pick it up. Put it in my pocket.

Have you ever felt yourself to be a figment of your own imagination?

Yes.

The questions come at Maria, one after another, until Nora just stops on one question and keeps repeating it over and over again, no matter how many times Maria answers, as if it holds some key.

Can you remember a time when you were really real?

There was a time when Maria could honestly say she hated white people. She felt she was allergic to them. She looked a lot like one of them, which made her understand how much they were getting away with every day of their lives. She flinched in white poeple's presence. She once overheard her mother saying to a friend, with a smirk of pride, that Maria had "that particular rage of the light-skinned individual." Probably the reason was that Maria was privy to what Gloria liked to call whiteyisms—those comments white people made about black people when they thought they were alone.

She lived that year in one of her college's ethnic-theme dorms. The black-theme house, Ujamaa. Every Thursday night was Cosby night. She and her friends hovered around the television as if they were watching a church sermon, hungrily taking in every detail of the most boring black family in America. Afterward they'd watch *A Different World*, laughing at the corny, hackneyed plots. It was such a sad relief to see these images, in such sharp contrast to the insidious television Negroes of their youth: the lanky and jive-talking (JJ), the fat and comforting (Florida, Nell), the stunted and orphaned (Webster, Arnold), or the benign tokens, roller-skates welded to their feet (Tootie). So night after night, in the lounge of Ujamaa, they hungrily ate up the sight of black people being rich, black people being normal, so normal they made Maria secretly want to vomit. It all felt a little pathetic to her, even then. It all suggested only that someday they would be as boring and vapid as white people. Someday Barbie and Ken would come in all the colors of the rainbow.

Can you remember a time when you were really real?

She carried a notebook with her everywhere that year, a notebook with a postcard of a gloomy-eyed James Baldwin taped to the cover. She permed her hair in the curly direction so that she looked more biracial. She'd have preferred to look like Whitney Houston, but she hadn't the moderate amount of melanin nor the doe eyes and button nose to pull it off, so she compromised at Jennifer Beals. The curls did soften her features, which she had always felt were unpleasantly angular. She put a sticker that said OPP on the door to her dormitory room and danced in a line to Digital Underground in the weekly "chill-outs" hosted by the Black Students Union.

Can you remember a time when you were really real?

The first time she had sex was in high school. She lost it,

so to speak, to an Argentinian Jew in his twenties. Was it rape? He was ten years older. She said, maybe, maybe, and he said, yes, yes, and fucked her. She watched his face over hers, his contorting expressions of pleasure, conscious that she was living inside an important scene in the movie of her life. Later, there was blood, and he looked nervous, stroked her arm. She wanted to get far away from him and his bodily fluids, the sticky innocence of them. Later, in college, she wondered if it was rape. It fit the definition of the women in her self-defense class. She'd said maybe and he'd done it to her anyway. But she didn't really feel it was rape. It was more like inserting a tampon. She hadn't liked it, and she'd been glad when it was over. Just like she was glad when her period was over. It was gross, in the same way. But she'd also known, even on the T ride home that night, that she wasn't any different than she'd been before he put it inside her, thrust around. And she knew too that whatever had happened then was not the cause of the crookedness inside of her.

Can you remember a time when you were really real?

Once, years ago, she'd read one of Gloria's old diaries. In an entry from the year Maria was born, her mother wrote: Maria is a strange baby. I don't think she loves anybody in particular. Or maybe she loves everyone equally. She squirms away from my embrace. She's perfectly cheerful, but I sense coldness.

Can you remember a time when you were really real?

Maria didn't know many other adopted children growing up. Gloria avoided the adoption community. There was a boy named Cedric in Maria's second-grade class who had been adopted from an Eritrean orphanage. His white parents never cut his hair. It was all locked up with plant matter stuck in it and Maria started at some point calling him Thidwick, after the warmhearted moose in the Dr. Seuss story who lets all the creatures of the forest make a home on his antlers. Gloria made Maria watch *Roots* that same year beside her on the couch. She talked the whole way through. She kept saying that it was a work of speculative fiction. I love Alex Haley as much as the next Negro, she said, I'm glad the brother's getting rich, but come on. There's no tracing our shit back. Once the boat leaves the port, don't bother. Just make friends with your shacklemate and try to stay alive.

Nora turns off the machine. Thank you, Maria—thank you for those memories. I'll be back in a few minutes with your test results. This should be—she pauses—very illuminating.

She strides across the room. Maria is alone in the Church of Scientology banquet hall. It is bare but for the framed posters hanging on the walls around her. One of them shows a family of three—mother, father, child—squatting with their arms around one another, grinning, superimposed beneath a blue sky and a silver skyscraper. The words above the family's head, italicized like scripture, read: *On the day we can fully trust one another, there will be peace on earth.*

The organization's gold emblem—half cross, half corporate logo—hovers in the air beside them. Another poster shows the profile of a woman in a military getup. *Only Clears and OTs will survive this planet, and we're the only ones who can make them!*

Nora is back, holding a stack of white pages. Her face is unreadable, impassive. She looks like she knows something. Maria squirms, uncomfortable now. Nora sits down across from her, the evidence in her hands. She lays out the pages. They are computer-generated charts and numbers, incomprehensible to the untrained eye. If nothing else, they look seriously damning.

Nora squints at Maria for a moment. She taps one of the pages.

This is blowing my mind, she says.

What is?

Your results. I mean, I actually can't believe it. These are your results. The machine doesn't lie.

Maria chews her lip. What's it say?

Nora leans forward so that Maria can't avoid meeting her gaze.

Listen closely to what I'm about to tell you. I need to tell you a secret. Are you listening?

Maria nods.

Nora cups her hands around her mouth and whispers: You can be anything you want to be.

Maria glances down at the pages. That's it? That's what it says?

And I mean anything. You could be running a Fortune 500 company. You could be a movie star. A banker. A doctor. A schoolteacher. You have that special something that makes people succeed in life. I don't know where it comes from, but some people—some small percentage of people on this planet—they have it. You have it, Maria.

Nora sits back in her chair, crosses her arms. Her blue eyes stare at Maria for a moment, sparkling.

I'll be honest. I'm a little jealous of you, Maria.

Thank you, Maria says. I mean, I'm sure you can be anything too.

But here's the thing, Nora says. She stares down at the indecipherable results printed out in front of her. I'm going to be truthful with you. There are these two areas on your chart that concern me. Frighten me, really. Look here. You are doing great in all these areas, and then suddenly the line dips—here and here.

Maria sees the sharp dips on the chart.

This here, Nora says, is deception. You're a deceptive person, Maria. Am I right?

I don't know. Not really.

And this here is belligerence. You are belligerent. Am I right? Are you belligerent?

That depends what you mean. What do you mean?

These two small things could destroy you. I don't say that lightly. When I said I was blown away, it was by your potential. But I can see here, right here, and here, and here too, why you haven't reached that potential. You haven't reached it, have you?

Maria shakes her head.

When I met you in college, I said, that's a girl who is going places. But you're not there, are you?

Maria says a soft no.

That's because you need to do the work to clear yourself. Do you know what it means to be clear?

Not really.

That's all it takes. Nora is off and running—talking, talking, talking. Maria listens to the jumble of words. At least they sound like words. She pretends to listen just to be polite, her leg jiggling. She might be more interested in Nora if she dressed better. Everyone in this place is dressed terribly. She doesn't know why they all stopped evolving, stylistically, after the eighties. Her eyes drift to Nora's wrist. She sees that her watch is a cheap Timex from 1989. Everything she's wearing is cheap from 1989, the year that invented cheap, the year they were in Self-Defense for Women together. It is as if time stopped there, on that mat,

Maria pushing Nora down to the ground. She stares at the watch. Sees that it says noon. Nora is still talking about how to get clear. Maria stares at the watch for a long blank moment before it dawns on her that she was on her way somewhere. That she's late. She has completely forgotten her appointment. Oma and Lisa are waiting for her in Bergdorf's bridal salon.

Oh my God, she says, and jumps up from her seat. She runs out of the Church of Scientology, passing all the smiling people. They call out to her, Are you okay? Can we help you with something?

She half expects them to tackle her but she gets out alive.

Outside, the hail has stopped but there is still a web of drizzle. She pushes through the swarm of midtown bodies as she runs, her purse slamming against her side, in the direction of Fifth Avenue. She does the math. It's four long avenues west and then two blocks north and then she will be there, but she will be terribly, horribly late.

When she finally arrives, out of breath, she is too afraid to check the time. She pushes inside through the gold revolving doors and stands for one bewildered moment staring at the makeup and perfume section, as bright and white as a hospital ward. She asks a security man in a suit for directions to the bridal salon. He points toward the elevators. She takes it to the fourth floor and steps off into a land of gilded mirrors and creamy white softness. The air is warm and too sweet, as if perfume is being pumped out of the vents. There are framed photographs hanging here too, but these ones are black-and-white portraits of brides smiling shyly over bouquets. No grooms. Just brides.

She sees a door marked Bridal Salon and opens it a crack to see Lisa and her grandmother sitting on a sofa on the far side of the room. They are holding cups of tea. They are tilted toward each other, whispering.

She steps inside and they both look up at her. Lisa wears a burgundy dress and her hair pinned up like a forties movie star. She looks elegant, old-fashioned, like Dorothy Dandridge.

Oma, tiny and delicate, is all dressed up too, in a blue polka-dot dress and black leather buckle shoes.

You're so late, Lisa says, a hard look in her eye. Lisa stares at her, studies her.

The subway, Maria says. It broke down.

Lisa is silent, frowning.

I am so sorry. Her voice is only a rasp.

Lisa is silent, her eyes cold, suspicious.

Oma is squinting at her, quizzically, as she holds Lisa's arm and teeters forward. She stands before her and points at her chest. What is this you wear?

Maria looks down to see she's wearing a sticker. Nora put it there. It says, *Welcome to the Church of Scientology*. Below that is her name scribbled in a Sharpie. Maria pulls it off and crumples it into a ball. She puts it in her pocket. Listen, she says. I can explain.

Lisa crosses her arms and sighs, rolls her eyes, looks into the distance.

No, Oma says, squeezing her arm. You explain nothing. You are here now and that's what matters. Look, we have work to do.

Maria turns to see what she had not noticed before. Five gowns displayed on mannequin bodies on the opposite side of the room. They stand in a row, headless, waiting for her to fill them.

The poet has an ordinary name—the most ordinary of names. Still, Maria knows how to find him. She knows what to look for. She remembers that he mentioned the street he lived on to Lisa and Khalil after the reading, while she was standing nearby. He also mentioned a Jewish deli downstairs where he ate most of his meals. When she looks it up in the white pages, there is only one person with his name living on East 10th Street above a Jewish deli. She is surprised at how easy it is to find him. Though she knows it's not true, she has come to think of him as a celebrity, somebody sought out by strangers.

It is late morning when she gets ready to leave. Khalil is on the phone with his business partner, Ethan, making plans to meet him in the city. The company they are launching together is beginning to take shape; it is all Khalil seems to talk about these days and it seems to Maria that he's always on the phone with Ethan or with him in person.

Maria clears her throat. Khalil turns around to face her, the phone held in the crook of his neck. She tells him she's going to work on her dissertation. He blows her a kiss, then turns back to his computer screen.

Maria stands for a moment, watching the back of his head, his Muppet-like silhouette against the glow of the monitor. She feels a heavy weight in her chest, a nameless dread. She wants to call to him, but she doesn't. Instead she turns and heads out into the cold, bright morning, leaving her bag of Jonestown materials behind.

She gets on a Manhattan-bound train, but instead of taking it all the way uptown, she gets off at West 4th Street. She walks to the used record shop where she saw the poet the week before. It's late morning. There are people in the record shop, not many, just a few. They are all of a certain type—grimy, with piercings and spiked hair. They stand around flipping through albums. She feels out of place in her black low-heeled boots, her plum lipstick, her diamond and sapphire engagement ring. She looks bourgeois—like an extra from *A Different World*—and the truth is, she doesn't belong to this grungy place, this punk music. She grew up listening to Whitney Houston, and she has never liked or known music outside of the mainstream. Being black and looking white was enough of a freak show.

The place carries mostly white rock but she finds a small section labeled R&B and Rap. It includes the music she listened to in high school. Kool and the Gang. Doug E. Fresh. LL Cool J. Her heart beats faster at the sight of Whitney Houston's first album—there she is, teen beauty queen with her hair slicked back, in a bathing suit, her lips shimmering. She stares at Whitney Houston for a long time. It seems to her she has always only ever wanted to look like Whitney Houston. She already owns this album, *Whitney*. She owns all of Whitney's albums. They are in a box somewhere.

She keeps flipping through the records until she comes upon an album by Stacy Lattisaw—*With You*. The singer looks about twelve on the cover, kind of dumpy and pale, not even close to Whitney Houston, but Maria remembers liking the song "Love on a Two-Way Street." She buys it and leaves the shop with her purchase and walks around the neighborhood hoping to bump into the poet. She walks for an hour and buys a hot dog. She sits on a bench in Washington Square Park taking bites of the hot dog and watching a group of homeless men.

One of the homeless men is leaning over, sifting through a backpack, searching for something. Another homeless man, smirking, tiptoes up behind him and kicks him as hard as he can right in the ass. The man flies forward and lands on his face. The one who kicked him begins to laugh, slapping his thigh, striding around, pointing and jeering. The one who fell gets up and begins to stomp and cry and rage like an angry child. The other keeps laughing, wiping joyous tears off his face, rocking back and forth holding his middle. The one who got kicked begins to chase him, shaking his fist, shouting violent obscenities. Maria chews her hot dog and watches. She hates the man who kicked the other one and hopes he gets hit by a car, but he only runs out of the park and disappears into the city. The other one stands at the gate staring out for a while but then just sits down on a bench and puts his face in his hands. She can't tell if he's crying or laughing. She cannot tell if they are friends or enemies. If it was a prank or an assault.

The worst prank she ever pulled was in college. Claudette was still her best friend, and it was their senior year. They liked to talk in British accents to each other. Claudette, so she hears, is living in England now, Brixton, maybe speaking like that full-time. At the time Maria had recently taken up with Khalil after he'd dumped his white girlfriend. Maria liked to joke that she was his transitional object. He was morphing into a race man before her very eyes. He had begun selling X T-shirts out of his dorm room. He'd become a columnist for the newspaper, their token black voice—though, as Claudette pointed out, he'd only known he was black for about ten minutes.

That week he'd published a column about embracing his black identity. He wrote that he'd grown up in a liberal, humanist, multiracial family, oblivious to his own blackness. He wrote that this kind of color-blind humanism had not prepared him adequately for the racism of the world. That he'd been robbed of his identity as a black man. He'd sold his birthright for that famed mess of pottage. Now, he wrote, he was claiming it. He was taking a long, probably permanent, break from whiteness. He didn't want to be a token, the some-of-my-best-friends-are-black kid, the cool black guy at the frat party. He said it had become exhausting, soul-wearying. He was no longer at war within his own beige body.

His column read like a manifesto, a stern rejection of all things muddy and mulatto.

He published it on a Thursday.

Saturday night, still high on born-again negritude, he went out to an Alpha Phi Alpha party with a group of friends. Maria stayed back at Ujamaa with Claudette. They smoked some reefer.

The joke was Claudette's idea. She said, Hey, I've got an idea. Let's make Khalil feel even blacker. Let's make him feel like the blackest man in the world.

Maria dialed his number and when his answering machine beeped she said in her best impression of a white boy: I read your fucking column, Khalil. Screw you, man. I'm sick of your bullshit. Me and the brothers, we're coming for you. We're gonna string you up by a dreadlock, man, and light you on fire.

She hung up, laughing. Claudette was rolling around in hysterics, marijuana-laced tears streaming down her face.

Their high wore off. Claudette grew sullen, quiet, seated on the bed, her now dull eyes fixed on a spot on the rug. Maria sat on the floor, cross-legged, eating a whole family-sized bag of Cheetos by herself. She felt sick. Claudette looked at her and told her to wash her face. Maria went to the mirror and saw that it too was covered in orange dust. Claudette said she was going home to sleep it off. They said goodnight.

Maria waited up for Khalil. She fell asleep at some point and woke up in the middle of the night. Khalil wasn't beside her the way he usually was. It was three in the morning. She went to check for him in his room on the second floor.

Halfway down the hall, she heard her own voice booming out of his open door. It was the message she'd left for him earlier, to amuse Claudette. She slowed her pace as she listened to her impression of a white man: We're gonna string you up by a fucking dreadlock, man, and light you on fire. Nigger boy.

Had she really said nigger boy? She didn't remember saying that, but she'd been stoned out of her mind. Chuckling a little, she started toward his room, but stopped at the edge of the door. Inside sat the entire leadership of the Black Student Union: the president, the treasurer, and six other members. It was three in the morning and they were all crowded into Khalil's single, huddled around his answering machine in solemn silence, listening to her message.

Oh fuck, Maria whispered. She looked down the hallway and was about to take off when Khalil spotted her.

Hi, babe, he said.

He rose and made his way through the crowd of bodies toward her, a strange expression on his face—half smile, half grimace. Did he hate her? Did they all despise her now? Would they take away her black card?

Khalil hugged her long and hard.

Hey, Maria, a girl seated on the bed said. What's up, girl. I guess you haven't heard about what happened. It's bad.

A boy beside her elaborated. Khalil got a message. Have you heard it?

Maria swallowed, shook her head, and stepped inside the room.

We think it was Sigma Nu, somebody said.

A girl named Cheryl, the president of the BSU, shook her head. The fucked-up thing is it was probably somebody who you sit next to in class every day. I mean, that's the part I cannot get around. This is our community too, guys. This is where we have to live.

Khalil looked at Maria. We're preparing a statement for the newspaper. You can help us out.

She sat down beside Cheryl. Okay, sure. I can help.

Later, after they'd finished preparing the statement for the student newspaper—after they'd finished speaking to the police—after they'd somehow gotten a direct line to the university president's home—after they woke the university president from his sleep and told him about the incident and after they played the recording of the voice message into his receiver at top volume—after they asked him, point-blank, if he was going to respond swiftly and decisively, or if he was going to go back to sleep in his bed of white privilege—after the president assured them that no, he was not going back to sleep, he was never going back to sleep, he was pulling on his pants right now—after the president assured them he was not part of the problem, he was on the right side of history, and that as soon as they let him off the phone, he was going to call his staff for an emergency meeting and get to the bottom of this nightmare—after the members of the BSU had trudged back to their own dormitory beds—after the sun had risen over the campus—Maria lay beside Khalil in his bed and let him make slow, solemn, revolutionary love to her.

As they lay side by side in postcoital stillness, she stared at Khalil's face. His jokey features held more gravitas somehow. There was a somber down-pull to his lips. He seemed to have turned, overnight, from boy to man.

He sat up beside her and scooted across the bed to the answering machine. He pressed play. Maria lay in a fetal position on the bed listening to her own deepened voice bellowing hatred and sick racial violence into the recently sexed air of the dorm room. She could just make out Claudette's high-pitched laughter in the background.

Earlier, a guy named Ralph, the treasurer of the BSU, had called attention to that background laughter.

Ralph said it sounded just like the laughter of a white boy named Billy from his early-morning statistics class.

When the message ended, Khalil turned to look at her. He wore an unfamiliar smile. Maria Janie Pierce, he said. Maria Janie Pierce.

He reached out, pulled her up and toward him, and stared into her eyes.

He knows, Maria thought. He's going to say he knows.

But instead he said: I want to marry you someday. I want to marry you and live with you in Brooklyn. I want us to have a tribe of children and a brownstone and a big hairy dog named Thurgood. He laughed, then continued. I want to give you a big life. I want us to be that couple. I want us to have it all, even that mess of pottage.

Maria felt uneasy. She swallowed. Asked him, What exactly is a mess of pottage?

He touched her cheek. Hey, I'm being serious. You don't have to fight this life. You don't have to fight being happy. Don't you want a big life?

Of course, she said. Of course.

They embraced.

In a small voice she told him that she loved him, and that yes, she wanted all of that too—that big life he'd described, the tribe of children, the brownstone in Brooklyn, the giant dog named Thurgood. She said she would learn how to make a mess of pottage—she would learn how to knit, even purl, whatever that was. Why not? She squeezed him tight, her eyes fixed on the now silent but winking answering machine in the corner.

Nobody ever caught the perpetrator. Billy from Introduction to Statistical Methods was a suspect but Billy had an alibi. Nobody could prove it was Sigma Nu either, though a cloud of suspicion hung over the house and they ended up hosting a social awareness day for the entire campus, complete with ethnic food kiosks and Kuumba dancers, in an attempt to clear their name.

The incident, as it were, launched a wave of protests that rippled through the campus, protests against institutional racism and the unbearable whiteness of being. The BSU began selling T-shirts and buttons on the plaza, including one that said, *Reparations—NOW!* Khalil designed and sold some of the T-shirts. The first ones he made were black and said in red Garamond across the middle: *The master's tools will never dismantle the master's house. Audre Lorde.* That design didn't sell as well as his second batch, which were cardinal red and said in black Garamond across the middle: *And still I rise. Maya Angelou.* Those were a hot seller, along with the buttons the BSU sold to white students wanting to show their support, the ones that said, in large letters, *Recovering Racist*.

The pinnacle of the year: Jesse Jackson of the Rainbow Coalition visited the campus and stood on a podium and told the students in a voice that sounded weirdly to Maria like Foghorn Leghorn that they were an inspiration to the nation. Keep hope alive! Jackson referred to Khalil in his speech only obliquely—"the young brother who was the target of this vicious attack"—but everyone in the audience knew who Jesse was talking about and people craned their heads to look at him, their eyes flashing with excitement. Khalil was famous. He got the fist bump wherever he went. Perfect strangers told him to "stay black, stay strong."

Maria had never seen the immersion phase of racial identity formation overtake a person more swiftly or more extremely than it did Khalil. The irony was that Maria got black points for her association with him. Nobody remembered that he'd played Hacky Sack or that he had been planning to live in the Enchanted Broccoli Forest, the hippie cooperative dormitory on the edge of campus. Nobody remembered that it was Maria who'd airlifted him out of there on a reconnaissance mission. Oh well. It didn't matter. Maria felt lucky she'd gotten away with the incident unscathed.

The only casualty was her friendship with Claudette. Over the days following the incident, Claudette stopped returning Maria's calls. When a week later she spotted Claudette at a booth at the Coffee House, seated with the LGBT crowd, Claudette only gave her a wan wave and slid down low in her seat, covered her face with a menu.

At first Maria thought Claudette was just waiting for the drama to simmer down—the way bank robbers in the movies temporarily split up after the heist, then meet up in the Bahamas later, when the coast is clear. But soon it became clear that she was distancing herself permanently from Maria. She waved when they passed each other on campus but kept moving. She always found an excuse not to stop and talk. She was late for her Harlem Renaissance seminar. She was rushing to an event in the LGBT Center. She was meeting friends—these loathsome new nameless friends!—in the city for a rave. She acquired as well—overnight it seemed—a homely girlfriend, someone Maria had never before seen in her life, a dishwater blonde whom Claudette kept propped on her bike's handlebars as though to shield herself from view.

The winter sunlight over Washington Square Park has a silver tinge. There is a Christmas garland, gold and garish, strung up along the streetlights and she thinks it looks so ugly without snow. She thinks she hears somebody whispering her name, but when she whips her head around there is nobody. She rises and begins to walk east. Before she knows it, she is there, on the street where he lives, at the address she has memorized.

She gazes up at the windows of the building but doesn't know which belongs to him. She has no plans, no plot really to get inside, but as she's standing there, a man comes out of the building and dashes past her, leaving Maria just enough time to grab the door before it closes. It feels inevitable. She steps inside the foyer and stares at the list of names and buzzers beside an intercom. She finds his last name beside 310. Just for kicks, really, she reaches out and presses the buzzer beside it. 309. Koehner in 309. She is startled when, a moment later, the door to the interior of the building clicks, the lock releasing. She pushes it open and steps inside.

She doesn't feel like herself. It's an expression, she knows, something people say. I don't feel like myself today. They are usually referring to illness. But there is an "I" who still exists when they say it. They don't feel like themselves. She doesn't feel like herself, doesn't even feel there is an "I" to not feel like. She imagines the one who she thought was herself has long since made it up to the carrel in the university library where she is sitting poring over notes on Jonestown. She thinks that she has split off from this girl and is not her anymore, but that the other girl still exists. She doesn't know when it happened.

She climbs the stairs, carrying the Stacy Lattisaw album in the bag at her side. Halfway up, she hears footsteps, somebody jogging down the stairwell in her direction. She stops, waits to come face to face with the poet. He will see her and know she has come here looking for him. But the man who comes around the bend is not the poet. He is an aging white-bearded hippie. He smiles.

'Scuse me, darlin', he says, and moves around her, past her, continues on his way, whistling.

She is both relieved and disappointed. She keeps climbing.

She hesitates on the third-floor landing. She has not made a plan. She has not come with a purpose. She had only hoped to bump into him at the record shop. But now she is here, inside his building. She understands she has crossed a line somewhere. And she understands too that it's not too late to turn around, to leave the building, walk to the subway, go up to the university, the library carrel she has been given, and sit reading about Jonestown as planned.

But she doesn't stop. She keeps moving toward apartment 310. The hall feels long, warped, oddly lit. She passes other doors, hears the muted sounds of the lives within. Someone plays the same five notes—the beginning to a song—over and over again on a guitar. Somebody else shrieks with laughter. A television is on, the sound of talk-show applause. A baby is crying. A small dog is yapping, furious.

She is almost to the end of the hall when a door beside her swings open. It is the door to apartment 309—the buzzer she pressed to get inside. A woman sticks her head out. A baby cries within. The woman has a phone in one hand, pressed to her ear. Her eyes are red and puffy as if she's been crying.

Thank fucking God, she says into the phone, Consuela just showed up.

Maria glances over her shoulder for Consuela. There is nobody there. The poet's door is two feet away from her. He is maybe two feet away.

The woman puts her hand over the phone and whispers to Maria, You got all my messages. Sorry to mess up your plans, but this really is an emergency. She pauses, eyes Maria up and down. You changed your hair, she says, frowning a little. It looks nice. Changes your whole face.

She disappears inside the apartment. Maria pauses before following her down a narrow hallway.

Oh, right, the woman is hissing into the phone. I forgot. You're such a mensch. You're such a goddamn good guy. Family man of the year. But I just can't do this anymore. You can't have us both. I'm not that stupid, Meryl. I mean women my generation, we got a raw deal. A raw fucking deal. You're a rotten lot—a bunch of macho pussies.

The woman claws at one side of her face, pulls the skin down so she looks like she's melting. She is so consumed by her passion that she seems unaware of Maria standing there, unaware of her baby crying in the other room.

The apartment is too hot. It's one of those buildings where they crank the heat up too high in the winter. Maria makes out the sound of a radiator hissing nearby as she stands in the middle of the room. She wants to tell the woman she's not Consuela. But now seems like the wrong moment to interrupt, given the intensity of the phone call. The woman is pacing, shaking her head, while the baby screams unattended in the other room. Maria looks around, wondering if the poet's apartment is the same size, the same layout. This one is decorated like so many others she has seen: a framed photograph of Billie Holiday looking anguished and on the verge of death; a forties poster of a worker woman flexing her muscle under the words *We Can Do It*. A Native American dream catcher. A kilim rug. A midcentury couch. She thinks she could walk into any apartment on this hall and find these same standard-fare objects. She wonders if the poet has any of them. She doubts it. She tries to imagine how he has decorated his place but can't imagine, and it seems poignant to her suddenly, the idea of him living all alone with actual furniture and objects he's purchased.

The baby is really screaming his or her head off in the other room.

Plastic toys lie scattered on the rug, a bouncy chair sits on a kitchen table. A half-full bottle of milk on the coffee table beside a plastic bowl with some congealed gray mush inside. The woman paces, shaking her head at what the person on the other end of the call is saying. She has cropped blond hair. Her body is still youthful, bony, boyish. She does not look like she was recently pregnant.

Maria can't take it anymore. She goes into the bedroom. The air is thick with the smell of urine, baby shit. The room has yellow walls decorated with stickers of farm animals, alphabet letters, and numbers. There is a white crib in the far corner from which the baby's screams come forth, loud, insistent. Maria goes to the crib and looks in and is surprised to see that the baby is Asian. She's dressed in a pink onesie.

Maria picks the baby up. Her diaper is full, bulging. She continues to scream, hysterical, as Maria takes her to the changing table and lays her down. She unsnaps her onesie and takes apart her diaper and sees that it is only pee but she has a bad diaper rash underneath. Her skin is red and chafing. It looks painful. Maria doesn't know babies, has never been a babysitter, but she picks up a tube of rash cream from the table and smears it around on the child's bottom and crotch. The baby stops crying and stares at Maria. She's a pretty baby now that she's not screaming. She has perfect baby features, bow lips, a set of shiny dark eyes. Maria hands her a rubber giraffe and she sticks it in her mouth, bites at it with her small nubs of teeth just forming.

Maria wonders if the poet is home. If he is, they might

be only feet from each other. She is overjoyed at the thought that he is so close, that they are in the same space, breathing the same air of the same building.

When she has cleared up the mistake, given the baby back to her mother, she will go to his door and knock. She will be bold. She will say, I was just in the neighborhood, thought I'd say hi. People used to do that, once upon a time—pop in on neighbors, unannounced. Of course she isn't really a neighbor, and it might seem strange that she's already in the building, but she is a friend. Sort of. A casual acquaintance. Not a total stranger. She tries to imagine the look on his face when he sees her. Will he be confused or amused, happy or irritated? She imagines he will look at her with wary amusement. She feels pretty certain he won't be surprised. It seems impossible that he has not felt it too— the pulse that beats between them. Seems impossible that he does not have the same notion that they are linked, through time and space.

The baby is calm now. Maria can no longer hear the woman's voice. She must have gotten off the phone. She's probably cleaning herself up, getting ready to go out. She picks up the baby and sniffs the top of her head and it smells sweet and pure, the universal baby head smell.

She carries the baby to the living room and says, aloud, Listen, there's been a mistake.

The living room is empty. The kitchen is empty. The apartment is empty. Maria's throat goes dry. Still holding the baby, she rushes to the window and looks out in time to see the woman walking down on the street. She's wearing a long gray down parka and high heels and holding her arm up to hail a taxi. Maria scrambles to open the window but it is painted shut and it doesn't matter anyway, because the woman has hailed a taxi. She slides inside and is gone.

■ ■ ■

Maria does this thing with her eyes, something she's been doing her whole life, where she makes them go blurry, then clear, blurry then clear. As she adjusts her eyes, she is half expecting the woman to reappear in the spot where she was standing, laughing and waving, because of course this was all some practical joke. But the woman is really gone and Maria is alone with the baby, who feels almost weightless in her arms.

The baby tugs at Maria's hair, makes cooing sounds.

Maria asks: What's your name? Where do you come from?

Her voice sounds strange to her, the bright false cheer of a missionary.

The baby stares back with solemn disdain.

Maria walks around the apartment with the baby on her hip, feeling bored already of being a nanny, though her shift has just begun. She notices with irritation that the woman left her with a mess in the kitchen. She wonders if this was in the job description or if it is just one of those things people do—hire a laborer to do one job, then hope they will do all this other extra stuff if you leave it around, undone. A pot sits on the stove with ramen noodles in it. There is a bowl holding rotten fruit—an orange with a fuzz of white mold on one side and a starkly black banana. A faint net of fruit flies hover above. Maria holds the baby with one arm while she throws the fruit and the ramen into a trash can and runs hot water in the sink, squeezes in some soap.

She sighs as she does so, mutters, Typical white woman shit—just leave it to the Latina.

The baby seems unhappy too and begins to squirm and whimper in her arms.

Maria abandons the kitchen cleanup and puts the baby down on the rug, gets down on her knees beside her, and dangles a toy—a small fuzzy white spider—in front of her face. The baby twists her body, grabbing for the toy. Once she has it in her hands, she loses interest and throws it down, begins to fuss, sucking on a fist, whimpering.

Maria picks up the baby, glimpses a bottle of milk on the coffee table, half-empty. She hands it to the baby and she sucks at it greedily, staring up at Maria with wary eyes.

After a while, her eyes flutter closed, the whites rolling up just before her lips relax and detach from the artificial nipple.

Maria carries the baby to the nursery-cum-bedroom and sets her down in the crib. The room still smells of baby shit, and maybe extramarital sex too. The shades are drawn and the bed is unmade, a rumple of dingy sheets. Maria goes to the far wall—the one the room shares with the poet—and places her palms flat against it, moving them around like a mime in an invisible box. She rests her ear against the cool whiteness and thinks she hears muted explosions on the other side—a television show. She stands closer, so that her whole body is pressed flat against the wall, her eyes squeezed shut. She knocks. Nothing happens. Knocks again. The television volume goes low and is followed by the sound of heavy male footsteps, a clearing throat. He heard her knock and thinks somebody is at his door. She hears him open his front door and she imagines him standing staring into the hallway. She laughs to herself at his confusion. It's like Ding Dong Ditch. She is tempted to go out there and surprise him, but doesn't. She hears his door shut. More footsteps. A moment later the sound of the television explosions returns.

When she thinks of the poet, she doesn't imagine their future—a relationship, a home, a union, a child. She only imagines the beginning, the moment before they are about to touch for the first time.

The poet is not a New Person. He could not be a subject in Elsa's documentary. He doesn't have mud-toned dreadlocks or octoroon-gray eyes or butterscotch skin. The poet is old-school—a brown-skinned black boy with a shaved head, a scar in his eyebrow. He has the body, the skin, the face that cabdrivers pretend not to see, that jewelers in midtown refuse to buzz inside. His body is the very reason they got those buzzers installed in the first place.

She wonders what kind of body the poet desires, what kind of skin and hair and face catch his eye in the street. Is it a black girl or a white girl? Is he a tit-man or an ass-man? Is he into boys or girls, or girls with appendages? Anything is possible. She knows nothing about him except her own desire.

Before Khalil, Maria had a type—a kind of body she desired. He looked nothing like Khalil or the poet. It's weird how sometimes she forgets that she was once, like Lisa, into white boys. What was it she overheard Gloria saying on the phone to a friend once when she was in high school? Maria loves her some white boys.

Not just any white boy. They always had the same look: olive skin, brown hair, sharp features, dark eyes. Israeli-ish, even if they weren't Israeli (though sometimes they were).

She remembers the last white boy. How could she forget? The last white boy in more ways than one. He died. He killed himself. Not literally, because some version of him still walks and talks on earth, but the white boy she knew is long gone.

Greg Winnicott. A long lean white boy from Darien, Connecticut. Tall—freakishly tall, like six foot four. He had the kind of male form Gloria liked to call a tall glass of water. Greg Winnicott. Bright-eyed. Articulate. Average intelligence. Firm handshake. Moderate Democrat. A perfectly good white boy. Maria knew him in college her freshman year, but in the years since they were together he has literally become somebody else.

Today, as far as she knows, he still goes by his new name. Goya, like the artist—like the beans. Every category about him has changed.

Once a few years back when she was bored, she scribbled a list on a pad of paper to work it all out in her head.

Greg Winnicott —→ *Goya Alvarez*

White —→ *Chicano*

Straight —→ *Queer*

Catholic —→ *Buddhist*

Premed —→ *Visual arts*

Thin —→ *Fat*

Anti–affirmative action —→ *Pro-reparations*

Moderate Democrat —→ *Green Party*

How such a thing happens—you have to go back to Stanford University, circa 1989. The era of the T-shirt revolutionary. The era of the anthology. The era of the individually designed major. The same year the school officially changed the term *freshman* to *frosh* so as not to alienate "half the sky." 1989. Both the beginning and the end, in other words, of everything.

She met Greg in her frosh dormitory. He lived on the second floor, she lived on the first. She desired him in the way she had always desired that type—she couldn't figure out where the hatred left off and the desire began.

There was a racial incident on campus that fall. Two drunk white students—responding to a widely publicized campus talk by a historian about Beethoven's black heritage—had defaced a poster of Beethoven to make him appear stereotypically Negroid and hung it up in the black-theme dorm. Giant Afro, big lips—the whole racist kit and caboodle.

In the midst of it, she found herself being professionally black—arguing with a bunch of white students in the hallway of her frosh dorm about why such crude racist imagery was offensive and why the school needed to take action. They seemed not to understand, which was astounding to her.

Maria called Gloria, ranting about the incident, expecting sympathy and encouragement. But Gloria sounded distracted. She was chewing on something, opening and closing a refrigerator door, running a bath. She kept bringing the conversation back to her homeopath, a guy named Chuck Whittle who had an office in his home in Somerville and who had helped her with her sinuses.

Maria received a letter from Gloria later that same week, written in longhand, purple script, offering her advice:

My dear Maria,

Don't hate white people. They can't help it. They have a learning disability. They need your compassion. They need accommodations. They are like preschoolers—their understanding of race is so basic. They can't be faulted for being uncomfortable with somebody who has what amounts to a graduate degree in race—that is, us. It's not fair for preschoolers to be placed in the same classroom with graduate students and be forced to compete. Pity them, Maria. Take their hands and explain very slowly and very carefully to them the truth of what you know, but with kindness in your heart. Have compassion for them, because not everybody starts on an equal playing field.

Love, Gloria

P.S. I am so eager for you to meet Chuck. He can really help you. He's got a remedy for everything!!!

Now Greg stood with a cluster of other white kids in a circle around her, trying to argue that the Beethoven poster was just a practical joke—insensitive, maybe, stupid, maybe, but not worthy of expelling the boys.

Greg said, People need to lighten up.

She exploded. She called him clueless—part of the motherfucking problem. Four-hundred-year-old rage surged through her.

He listened with shimmering doe eyes to her rant.

When she was done, she immediately wanted to have sex with him. So she did.

She began to date Greg, but with an appropriate sense of self-loathing. He accused her of being the queen of ambivalence. She couldn't deny it. She hated the way they looked together. She would sometimes glimpse herself with him in a reflection—holding his hand while they walked through Palo Alto, or kissing him outside a party, or sitting on his lap—and feel a literal surge of bile rising to her throat. They looked cute together. They looked like a cute white couple. She looked like she belonged on his lap.

She told Greg not to get too attached: told him she just wanted to sleep with him, not settle down with him or anything—which, it turns out, was the key phrase to winning any man's heart.

Greg mentioned from time to time that he had a Chilean grandmother. Maria was not impressed. Did you even know her? she asked. He shook his head. So then what does that mean to you? He didn't have an answer.

When they watched a movie together in bed where the black characters were doing some Stepin Fetchit routine, she watched his face to see if he would laugh. When he did laugh, she pressed pause and asked him why he was laughing. She policed his chuckles.

■ ■ ■

Around campus that same year, Maria noticed a boy out of the corner of her eye—a miscellaneous black kid surrounded by white kids. She saw him playing Hacky Sack, his Basquiat dreadlocks flopping around on his head. He looked familiar to her, uncannily so. She couldn't remember how or why, but she knew that boy from somewhere.

Meanwhile, Greg was getting clingy. She asked him not to hold her hand when they walked around campus together. She said she didn't like PDA, but they both knew that was not the real issue. She told him not to get too comfortable. She said she could never have children with a guy like him; she'd feel trapped. He mentioned his Chilean grandmother, and she sighed. You're just not getting it, are you?

One night, after too much to drink, she paced around his dorm room, naked, his cum still inside of her, ranting like Huey P. Newton about the trouble with white people. He listened, lying long and lean and golden tan before her.

Do you even love me? he asked when she was done with her speech.

As much as I can.

He stared at her, lips parted, as if something was dawning on him.

She said she had to go. She needed to attend a BSU meeting in the lobby of Ujamaa. It was an important meeting— they were voting on something essential, she couldn't remember what.

He asked if he could join her.

She said, You have to identify as a person of color to even attend the meetings.

He put his face in his hands. She felt a wave of pity move through her.

Um, are you okay? she asked.

He glanced up wearing a pained smile. I was just thinking about something my dad once told me. He was coaching my football team and he said to me, Son, when you can't decide, you end up with nothing.

That's sweet, Maria said. I can just picture it. Father-son bonding at a football game. How despicably American.

She began to put on her clothes. Listen, she said, I realize you think that I, quote unquote, can't decide, that I'm some tragic mulatta, betwixt and between. The queen of ambivalence. And maybe that idea is a big turn-on for you. I don't really know. But the truth is, Greg, I can decide and, actually, I have decided. I could never settle into this. She waved her arm around at his dorm room. I could never really feel, I don't know, at home with you. Don't take it personally.

Greg spoke. His voice was calm.

Last night, he said, while you were out with Claudette, I went to a party at the Phi Delt house. I didn't tell you because I knew you would freak out, call me a frat boy or something. I just had to get out of this room. Anyway, Sally Eubanks tried to kiss me at a party. When I told her I had a girlfriend, she said, You mean Sacagawea? I told her your name was Maria. She said that she and other girls in our dorm have nicknamed you Sacagawea.

Maria was dressed now, brushing her hair in the mirror, a smile on her face she couldn't explain.

Sacagawea, she said. That's some fucked-up bullshit. I should report that to the administration.

Oh Jesus, Maria. Cut it out. That was just her jealousy talking. I know it's hard for you to imagine but she wanted me. Anyway, I'm talking about you and me now. Us. Anyway, she asked me why I was so hung up on you. She said, Why is a guy like you chasing after such an odd, twisted girl? That's what she called you. "An odd, twisted girl." I tried to defend you, Maria, but I couldn't really give her a good answer.

So don't defend me, Maria said, turning to look at him. Anyway, there is no us. There never was.

She left to go to her meeting. As she walked across campus, she tried to feel sad, or happy, or anything, but she felt numb. She sat in the back of the BSU meeting, silent, listening to students ranting about the lack of diversity in some required frosh survey course. She listened but didn't really hear the words people spoke. She raised her hand when they had a vote, something about bell hooks, then left in a daze.

She woke that same night alone in her single bed in her own single room in Otero. She felt the presence of something in the room. Somebody. She'd felt this presence before. It was back. A rhythmic beating, like a heart that was not her own. She sat up and turned on the light. She could hear sighing in her room. It was lurking in the corner. It was a gray shape, a creature—an ever-restless pet. It had entered the space while she was sleeping and was waiting for her. It shifted positions as it watched her, breathing. She was afraid to look at it directly. She said aloud, her eyes fixed on her desk, Go away. Then she turned off the light and lay alert as a soldier until morning.

She didn't see Greg for a long time—weeks—after their breakup. She did notice somebody else, the strangely familiar boy she'd seen before. The boy with the Basquiat hair. Mr. Miscellaneous. He was never alone. He moved with an entourage of straggly-haired, alterna-white people—the ones who lived at the edge of campus in the Enchanted Broccoli Forest. The ones who were rumored to Dumpster dive behind restaurants for their dinners so as not to waste the earth's resources.

Mr. Miscellaneous didn't look like them, really. He looked like he bathed, for one thing. Plus, he was more stylish, in horn-rimmed nerd glasses and a Bad Brains T-shirt. But he seemed necessary to them somehow, a necessary part of their flora and fauna. It became a game for Maria, to spot Mr. Miscellaneous around campus. There he was, playing Hacky Sack in the Quad. There he was, standing on top of a picnic table outside of the Coffee House, tapping a glass with a spoon as if about to make an important speech to a bunch of laughing friends. There he was, flirting—repulsively—with a barefoot and braless blonde in a peasant skirt, a ring in her nose.

He lived in Roble, the biggest frosh dorm on campus, which was fine and well. But the important thing was this: After freshman year, you got to declare your identity, your allegiance, based on where you applied to live. Some went to live in theme dorms, where they immersed themselves in blackness or Chicano-ness or Asian-ness or queerness. Others went to live in fraternity houses, or in the co-op houses that lined the campus, and these too, Maria knew, were ethnic-theme houses. White ethnic-theme houses.

Maria saw Mr. Miscellaneous going down a bad path. He needed somebody to stop him before it was too late.

She longed to talk to him, but it wasn't like the longing she'd felt toward other boys. Was it romantic, or something else? She couldn't say—only that she wanted him to know she existed.

Thanksgiving break she could not afford to fly east. Gloria had no money, was living hand to mouth until her dissertation was finished.

Maria's dormitory mostly emptied out except for a few international students. She ate her holiday dinner in the dining hall with an Uzbeki boy and a Malaysian girl who played footsie and made eyes at each other over the prepackaged turkey dinner and ignored her. She excused herself before dessert and went back to her room. She lay down on her bed, but the moment she hit the mattress she heard it—a sigh. She swallowed. Hello? There was silence. Still, she felt it. A trembling. A breathing, almost imperceptible, in the room with her. She was too scared to move. She sensed somebody was under the bed. She could just make out a second heartbeat. She lay very still. Her eyes welled with tears. It had come for her, whatever it was. She heard it shift. She leaped up and raced out of her room, slamming the door behind her.

It was early evening. She ran for a long time across the deserted campus, her huarache sandals slapping the pavement, her heart pumping. She could feel it—a shadow, a throbbing presence—right behind her. It was chasing her. Finally, she could run no more. She looked back, panting, and saw there was nothing there.

She caught her breath and sat on a bench. The Mission buildings were bathed in a fading peach and orange sunset.

The campus was devoid of students. She had never seen anything quite so beautiful or quite so empty.

But then she heard it, a strange and distant sound: a skidding, rolling, scraping.

She stood up. There was something there. She followed the sound through the fading evening light. It grew louder and louder until she found herself at the edge of the Quad.

There, alone, in front of Mem Chu, was Mr. Miscellaneous. The whitest black man in the world. The blackest white man in the world. The sound was his skateboard. She watched him from the shadows of the poli-sci building as he did slow rolls back and forth across the empty space. His arm was in a sling.

Maria felt something fluttering to life in her chest—a widening, a clarifying, an openness. She saw a future she'd never before been able to imagine—her and him, seated on a wide porch together, glamorous into old age, like Ruby Dee and Ossie Davis—which was another way of saying that anything and everything seemed possible.

He didn't see her yet. He attempted a fancy move and flew off the skateboard, caught his fall, stumbled, and righted himself. Maria stepped out of the shadows into the Quad. He looked up and laughed.

I thought I was alone.

Me too.

He shrugged. It's just the internationals and us.

She eyed him, saw that up close his features were quite

striking. He looked both entirely black and entirely white. While she had melted into a Mexican, in him both parts were held together in a kind of balance.

She coughed into her hand, tried to look casual—asked him how he'd injured his arm.

Mosh pit.

Mosh what?

You're kidding, right? He squinted at her. Pogoing? Punk?

Wait, she said. Does this involve white music? I don't listen to white music.

He looked taken aback. What's white music?

Same thing as black music, only white.

Oh.

He was studying her face. Who are you?

I'm Maria, she said. I feel like we've met before.

I'm Khalil, he said, squinting now, as if he thought he remembered her too.

■　■　■

And then, before she knew it, they were one. Attached at the hip. Maria and Khalil: King and Queen of the Racially Nebulous Prom. They held hands everywhere. She led him to the places he needed to go, places he'd never gone before: the lounge in Ujamaa, with its weekly conversations about everything from interracial dating to whether rap music was misogynist. She brought him to his first BSU meeting. She brought him to Cosby night. She brought him to a performance of the Kuumba dancers, the quasi-African student dance troupe. He learned about apostrophes in newfangled, old-fangled places and double vowels and the wit and wisdom of Ron Karenga. He attended with Maria his first step show, where with saucer eyes he watched five clean-cut pledges stomp around in purple and gold—chanting over and over again the words of the age-old Negro spiritual: Proud to be an Omega, Proud to be an Omega. She brought him to his first late-night chicken and waffles in an Oakland juke joint. She taught him at what point at a party he needed to start chanting, *The roof, the roof, the roof is on fire.*

At times Maria felt like Vanna White sweeping her hand across the brand-new kitchen set, saying, All this could be yours. Khalil had seen the dark and he wasn't going back. He cut the barefoot hippie girl loose, along with the gang from the Enchanted Broccoli Forest.

Sophomore year Khalil and Maria moved together into Ujamaa; they each scored a single, hers on the girls' floor, his on the boys'.

In bed at night, Khalil wanted to know about Maria's past. He fell asleep easily beside her, listening to her tales. She thought maybe he had narcolepsy. She learned to talk anyway, whether his eyes were open or closed. She told him everything, including that she'd had a fling with a white boy in her frosh dorm. When she said it like that, it seemed true—that it was just a fling with a white boy.

And anyway, it didn't matter how she described it. Because soon enough Greg was no longer a white boy. He was no longer Greg.

He was Goya.

■ ■ ■

The light in the room has shifted toward darkness. The baby is still asleep. Maria thinks she should call Khalil, tell him that she has been held up, that she will be home late. But she cannot explain what has happened. It won't make sense.

In the half light, Maria examines her hand, the diamond and sapphire ring. It looks like somebody else's hand, a woman she would like to become someday. A fiancée. The hand of a special somebody. The hand of an emergency contact on an official form. The ring is evidence that she is part of this tribe—herself, Khalil, Lisa, their friends—a tangle of mud-colored New People who have come to carry the nation—blood-soaked, guilty of everything of which it has been accused—into the future.

Panic tightens in Maria's chest. She regrets every choice she made today. She misses Khalil. She wants to return to their apartment. She feels trapped in this apartment. She feels trapped because she is, quite literally, trapped. She doesn't want to be Consuela. Doesn't want to be in this other woman's dingy space taking care of the baby. Babies, she realizes now, are a kind of hell. Cute for five minutes. Cute when they are asleep with their butts in the air. But the rest of the time? Hell. The worst is the idea of paying money to get one from overseas. She can't imagine paying for this kind of indentured servitude. Paying good money to be a beast of burden. Babies should be foisted on you by forces out of your control. If there was any sense in the universe, babies should always be an accident, a mistake, a lusty night involving alcohol and drugs and a broken condom.

The baby of course will wake up. She dreads it. She wants to go home before this happens, to her small, culturally elite apartment in Brooklyn, to eat Moroccan tagine with Khalil in front of a movie, maybe *Chameleon Street* for the umpteenth time. The movie is misogynist—Khalil always makes sure to mention this detail—but even so, he can't deny its genius.

She won't go, though. She knows she cannot abandon the baby. Nora Convey and the machine may have been right about her flaws—it may have been true that she wasn't yet living up to her potential—Gloria may have been right that she was "into white boys" and Sally Eubanks may have been right that she was an "odd, twisted girl." She may be a lot of things, but she is not the kind of girl to walk away from a helpless baby.

The window. She goes and stares longingly down onto the street. It is Saturday night and the East Village is abuzz with activity. She feels a bitter jealousy toward the people on the other side of the glass, with their whole nights ahead of them, babyless. There is a fire escape just beyond the glass. She tries the window and finds this one isn't painted shut. It slides up easily. She leans her head out and inhales. It is really winter. She catches that in the air. It is December and the Thanksgiving hysteria has already given way to the Christmas hysteria. She hears a Salvation Army bell ringing, drearily, into the sea of atheists. She closes her eyes and listens and it is as if she were in another time, any time, the sound of that bell ringing, the voice begging for charity, is so timeless. When she opens her eyes, a new calm has come over her. She leans out to look at the apartment next door. A light glows softly from the poet's window. She is so close. She hesitates only for a moment before climbing out onto the metal landing. The air is crisp and stings her skin, reviving her, washing away the warm funk of baby-minding. She thinks she will just take a look inside. What the hell, she's come this far and gotten this close. She begins to edge along the fire escape until she is right outside his apartment. She will just peek inside. She will just get a sense of how he lives and then she will go back to the baby, to her duties as Consuela.

His window is half open. Inside, it is the exact same layout as the apartment next door. It is sparsely furnished: a lumpy blue couch, makeshift bookshelves, a little wooden table with one chair for eating. How poignant, she thinks, to imagine him eating alone at that little table. The poet in his lair. She feels oddly peaceful sitting there, looking in, when the door to the bathroom swings open and the poet steps out, zipping up his pants. She sits back against the brick wall, her heart slamming into her chest. She can hear the sound of a toilet running behind him. She hears his footsteps. A moment later, she hears his voice.

He's not far from the window. She glances in, hoping the darkness will conceal her. His back is turned away from the window, but he's only a few feet away. He's talking on the phone to someone.

Where do you want to meet?

—

Uh-huh. I know the place.

—

Ten minutes.

—

He laughs. Okay. I'll be sure to bring it.

He hangs up and stands still for a moment. She wonders if he can feel her eyes on his back, if he senses that someone is watching him. Then he walks away, puts the phone back in its cradle by the television, grabs a jacket off the sofa, and puts it on. He takes a brush and weirdly runs it over his bald head. Pulls a stick of lip balm out of his jeans pocket and rubs it on.

It is the Chapstick that does it. It gives her a very bad feeling. A sick feeling, really, that he is going out on a date. Going to meet a woman. She watches him check for his keys and wallet, then switch off the light and head out the door. She sits there, hugging her knees, staring down at the street below. A few minutes later she sees him emerge on the sidewalk and walk with his head tilted down toward Third Avenue, then disappear around the corner.

He forgot to close his window. Not a wise move. She thinks about how people get robbed all the time in this city. They leave their window open a crack, and next thing they know, their entire life is being hawked from a blanket on Second Avenue.

She sits for a while, thinking. And when she moves forward, she is intending to close his window, but instead she opens it wider.

* * *

She doesn't turn on the light. She can see well enough in the dark. It smells better than it does next door. It smells of soap and coffee. There isn't much food in his cupboards. Or the refrigerator. A Dannon yogurt, a carton of coffee creamer, a box of Stoned Wheat Thins, a bag of cashews, a few bottles of fancy beer. All a poet needs to live and breathe. She removes a beer, twists it open, and takes a long chug. It's delicious, high quality—India pale ale. She strides around holding it in her hand, feeling somehow not like herself. For a moment she feels that she is the poet himself.

His apartment is neat. She remembers how clean the poet looks. He always looks freshly showered. She imagines his neck smells good. She sips the India pale ale as she moves around, picking up objects, turning them over. A clay child-sized handprint signed Derrick, maybe a friend's child or a nephew. She hopes he doesn't have a child. She doubts it. A snow globe with Paris inside. She shakes it, smiles as she watches the flakes fall around the Eiffel Tower. She runs his brush through her hair, pleased by the sight of the strands she leaves behind, not removing them. She goes to the bathroom, sits down and pees in the darkness, decides not to flush. She brushes her teeth with his toothbrush, minus the paste, then rinses it off and puts it back in its holder.

She enters the bedroom. A computer monitor glows in the darkness. She expects to see lines of half-finished verse on the screen, but the screen holds a frozen image from a video game. He has paused mid-game. He has 256 points.

His bed is queen-sized, with a flowered comforter he's

partway pulled up in a halfhearted attempt at making it, which seems touching to her somehow. She puts the beer down on his nightstand and climbs onto his bed and hugs the pillow, inhales his boyish scent. Desire courses through her.

She liked to have sex with Greg. That was all they shared, really. Other than that, she despised him.

But in all the years they've been together, she has never really enjoyed sex with Khalil. In bed, they're like cousins. It has always been that way.

The first time she and Khalil kissed, she had the thought: One of us is gay. Either he's gay or I'm gay. Because it felt strange like that. And it made her think of something her friend Claudette once said. Claudette described what it was like to be a dyke and to kiss a boy. Claudette said it felt like kissing her brother or cousin, somebody you would feel no erotic tension toward. She said every time she'd tried kissing a boy she always thought: There is a tongue moving inside my mouth. Like, there is a bug crawling on my leg. It wasn't quite that lifeless with Khalil, but she has felt none of the warm rush of desire she felt toward Greg.

Though they've never touched, she feels pretty certain she would enjoy sex with the poet. The attraction feels real. She kisses his pillow now, strokes it, and imagines it's his face. She can almost get turned on. She can almost imagine that she is part of the scene in her head, not just watching. She lies there for a while, just holding the pillow in her arms, feeling almost satisfied with just this, his smell, his sheets. It's almost enough. Distantly, she is aware of a familiar sound. It is like a buzzing, but not. An irritating, grating sound. She tries to ignore it but it persists. The worst sound she's ever heard. Like a car alarm going off in the street, only worse.

She puts her hands over her face. Of course. It is the baby, alone in the dark fetid bedroom, crying, a small gray shape.

Sighing, Maria rises and heads back through the dark apartment to the window. She climbs out onto the fire escape and closes the window behind her. She starts to crawl across the metal to the other apartment, but glimpses a bearded young white man standing on the fire escape directly across the street. He wears only boxer shorts and a large blanket draped over his shoulders. He is smoking a cigarette and watching her. She fixes a silly grin on her face and raises a hand, as if to say, it's okay, I'm crawling out of one dark window and into another, but I'm not an intruder. She knows that if she looked anything like the poet this man would call the police right now. The cops would come and blow her away with no questions asked. But she doesn't look like the poet, so the bearded guy just smiles and waves back, as if what she's doing is normal—or a joke they are both in on. She lowers herself back inside the woman's apartment and goes to the baby, who is shrieking, hysterical now. Maria leans over the crib and says, I'm here. At the sight of Maria's face, the baby screams harder, her eyes alarmed. Maria reaches down to pick her up and holds her, jiggles her, says in what she hopes sounds like a faint Spanish accent, It's okay, Consuela's here. No cry, baby, no cry. Consuela is here.

■ ■ ■

The woman, she learns from the unopened gas bill on the counter, is Susan. And the best news she's had in a while— she's left an extra set of keys for Consuela on the hallway table. Maria checks that they work, then heads out into the night, clutching the wet-eyed baby in one arm, dragging the stroller behind her with the other.

On the street, strangers ogle Maria. At first she is confused by the stares, the smiles—she thinks there is something stuck to her face. She wipes her mouth as she walks. Then she realizes that it is about the baby. It is the baby they have been smiling about. It is the fact that Maria has a Chinese baby girl and she is not Chinese. She's getting do-gooder smirks because of this baby.

A young man with blazing blue eyes says, as they pass, God bless you.

A woman at a crosswalk points at the baby and says to the man at her side, Oh wow, we were just talking about adoption.

Gloria used to say that when a baby doesn't look like it came from your body, you become a specimen for the world's study. You become a Rorschach test—a walking, talking inkblot. People feel free to discuss you and all that you represent. When there is a gap—between your face and your race, between the baby and the mother, between your body and yourself—you are expected, everywhere you go, to explain the gap.

On legal forms, Gloria was her mother, but Maria never called her Mother or any of its variants. She only ever called Gloria by her name. Gloria said she didn't believe in bullshitting a child. She never wanted there to be bullshit between them.

Gloria told Maria the whole story of her adoption by the time she was seven years old. She had adopted Maria after breaking up with a man—a fellow graduate student she would only ever refer to as H—who had wanted her to stand behind him at protests, and type up his dissertation, and serve him dinner and wash the dishes and bear him some children and write her own dissertation in between folding laundry. He'd seemed attracted to her in direct proportion to how well she disappeared into their backdrop.

Gloria was in her midthirties then and just beginning her graduate program. She knew there were many black babies languishing in the system, unwanted. She put in a request for a healthy black infant girl. It was only a few months before she got a call from the agency saying they had one available. The baby was only a few weeks old and her name was Maria. She came from the Cane River in Louisiana. They didn't have much more information than that except that she was in the care of a Catholic orphanage now—the Saint Ann's Infant and Maternity Home in Maryland. Gloria dropped everything and drove the eight hours to collect her child.

During Maria's first six months of life, Gloria waited for her to change—for the baby to shed her straight hair and to darken up. But it never happened. Her hair never got kinky. Her skin remained high Cotton Club yellow. It was not until Maria was ten months old that Gloria accepted what was clear: the baby was a one-dropper, that peculiarly American creation, white in all outward appearances but black for generations on paper.

When they went out for walks around Cambridge, people on the street and in the park assumed Gloria was the nanny, taking care of a baby for some invisible white lady. After such encounters she found herself aware, with an almost scientific detachment, of the baby's skin and hair, the shape of her features. And in those moments she could not help but think of her own mother, who had spent a lifetime caring for white babies so that when she got home, she was too tired and depressed to care for her own children. She could not help but think of all the women whose backs she'd stood on to get to this place, this lonely tower overlooking the river, and how she was going to care for this pale child all the days of her life, a child who—one-drop rule be damned—looked just like all the other babies who had been nursed by black women through the ages.

But she also knew that it was too late to send the baby back to where she'd come from, too late for her to request a darker baby. Because she already loved the baby, the way you do love babies when you are the only thing keeping them alive.

■ ■ ■

Maria has walked ten minutes north, ten minutes south, ten minutes west, ten minutes east—has looked through the window and doorway of every eating and drinking establishment in the vicinity—but the poet is nowhere to be found. Where has he gone? Who was he going to meet? What does the other woman look like?

For a flash, she thinks she sees him—a shaved-head black man stepping out of Pearson's Texas BBQ with a fat blond woman on his arm. Maria watches, a cry forming in her throat—but when he turns his head she sees it is a different black man, much older, with sagging jowls, a potbelly, baggy eyes. Nothing like the poet.

It's getting cold. She is tired. She wants to be rid of the baby. She's bored of the nanny shtick. She doesn't want to go back to Susan's apartment either. The place depresses her.

She finds a payphone and calls Khalil. He answers on the second ring. To her surprise, he doesn't sound worried or upset.

Hey, babe, he says. She can hear John Coltrane playing

in the background. He tells her that she had a phone message today from the Beach Plum Inn on Martha's Vineyard wanting to discuss the block of rooms they've reserved for the wedding party. He's saved the message for her on the answering machine.

She twists the phone's metal cord around her wrist.

Where are you? he asks.

She pauses. I'm on campus, she says. Just outside the library.

Oh, right. So you want to just meet me there?

Where?

Don't tell me you forgot. Dhaka. For Lisa's birthday dinner.

Dhaka. A Bangladeshi restaurant not far from where she stands. She'd forgotten about the dinner. She feels a twinge of irritation. It seems to her they are always eating Bangladeshi food together. Whenever they go to Bangladeshi restaurants in the city, Khalil insists on eating with his fingers. Maria has asked him to stop eating with his fingers, but he says it's how they eat in Bangladesh.

Of course, she says now. I'll be there.

He asks her if she picked up the present.

She hesitates. She remembers him shouting something to her this morning about a present.

Yes, she says. I have the present. She glances at the baby, who throws back a look of pure shade.

■ ■ ■

Susan is home. Her parka lies strewn in the hallway. Maria, out of breath from the walk up the stairs, kicks it aside. She heads down the hall to find Susan seated in the glow of the television. Her face is puffy, her mascara smeared. She watching a kid's movie. *Beethoven.*

We're home, Maria says in a bright, false voice. She is carries the baby to Susan and stands over her, waiting for her to take the baby back.

Susan looks up and forces a small brave smile.

Hi, darling girl, did you have a good day with Consuela?

Her smile falters a bit when she looks at Maria.

You did something. What is it? Something's different.

Maria thinks quickly and begins to spin a circle with the baby, in an effort to blur her face. She doesn't know if what she's done here is illegal. She thinks it might be. She says, as she spins the baby, letting her hair whip around her features, We had a blast, didn't we?

The baby doesn't smile or laugh. She looks judging. Maria stops spinning and stands with her face tilted down over the baby, hair falling like Sheila E.'s over one eye. She stands at an odd angle away from Susan.

Be a doll, Consuela, Susan says, stifling a yawn, and put June to sleep before you go? I had a hell of a night. I'm feeling—low. She reaches forward and picks up a crumpled ball of tissues from the coffee table, blows her nose.

Maria grunts her assent and carries the baby into the bedroom and begins to change her diaper.

June. So her name is June. It seems to her that adopted Chinese girls are so often named June. Or May. Just like interracially adopted black boys so often seem to be named Elijah. And biracial daughters of poor white mothers are so often Jasmine or Tiffany. She always hopes for something less predictable, and rarely gets it.

June watches her as she works. She is the most discerning baby Maria has ever encountered. Maria is glad she can't talk. She finishes changing her and attempts to get her to go to sleep. She paces the room, jiggling her, rocking her, singing Whitney Houston and Diana Ross hits. Gloria used to complain to the Afro-Am department secretary, Loretta, about Maria's taste in music: She won't listen to real music, she would say. She likes skinny crossover divas with cocaine problems, I mean, just crap.

Maria's and Gloria's most vicious fights were about music. During Maria's preteen years their apartment became a war of music. Maria would go and lock herself into her tiny bedroom that was really a converted pantry and put on her Walkman and try to shut out Gloria and Loretta, their wah-wah middle-aged voices at the kitchen table. The walls of her little room were covered in magazine tear-outs of Whitney and Diana and Michael, the holy trinity of medium brown, apolitical, smiling, gorgeous faces. She hated especially when Gloria listened to Aretha—she got a little too into it and Maria found it embarrassing. Gloria would squeeze her eyes shut and dance around, hand waving in the air, like she was really at a concert. Maria would say, Oh my God, stop being such a freak, and she'd move to turn down Aretha, and Gloria would lunge at her and turn it up instead, to messianic volume. They would tussle over the stereo knob. There was a certain theater to it all. And now Maria understands, in retrospect, that they both secretly enjoyed those fights. It was when they were slamming doors and expressing the utmost in loathing toward each other that they felt most like real mother and daughter.

The baby—after what feels like a sadistically long stare-down—does finally fall asleep. One moment she's awake, the next her eyes flutter closed. Just like that.

Maria returns, relieved, to the living room, eager to get the hell out of there.

Susan is still sitting where she left her, illuminated only by the flickering life on-screen. She stares expressionless at the made-up world of family and dog.

Okay, she's asleep, Maria says, in a strange accent that she recognizes doesn't sound remotely Hispanic.

Do you want to know something? Susan says, her eyes fixed on the screen. I think June is more bonded to you than she is to me.

That's not true, Miss Susan.

Yes, it is true. And it's okay. I get it. I get that I'm not the best mother. She's eight months old and already I can see I'm fucking it up. Someday she'll probably hate me. She'll say I did everything wrong and that I should have never adopted her and she'll probably be right. If she's smart, she'll write a book about me, saying how I failed her, sell a million copies. People love to see a single mother fail. But goddammit, Consuela, motherhood isn't easy. It is not what you think it's going to be, you know? I mean, I forgive my mother every mistake she ever made. Nobody tells you how hard it's going to be. And I haven't even gotten to the bitchy teen years. So it's okay if she loves you more, Consuela. You're probably doing a better job with her than me.

Thank you, Miss Susan.

Anyway, at least she's not rotting in a Beijing orphanage. At least she's here. She's in America.

That's true.

Susan stretches out prone on the couch and says, Come sit down, Consuela. Take a load off. You don't have to rush off yet, do you?

Maria pauses, then goes and sits down in the corner of the sofa, as far from Susan as she can. She keeps her face fixed forward. She can feel Susan looking at her and she tries to make her face appear older, bored and tired, like somebody who takes care of babies for a living.

You really did lose weight, Susan says. You look good.

Thank you, Miss Susan.

Susan lifts her foot and puts it in Maria's lap. Can you do me a huge favor and rub my feet like you did that time? You wouldn't believe how much I walked tonight. In heels!

She places her foot in Maria's lap. Her heel is calloused, the pink polish is chipped, her toenails long and thickened. Maria stares at the foot. She can feel Susan watching her and she feels it is a test. She picks up Susan's foot and begins to stroke it.

Harder, Susan says. Like you did before.

Maria begins to rub it harder, and when she glances at Susan, indeed her eyes are closed and her face has relaxed in pleasure.

You've got healing hands, Consuela. Has anyone ever told you that? I don't know what I'd do without you.

Thank you, Miss Susan.

Mmm. Yes. Right there.

Like this?

Yes. Just like that. She takes a deep relaxed breath, then says, Have you been taking English lessons?

Yes, Miss Susan.

I can tell. Your accent is almost gone. I didn't even notice it fading. You sound almost American.

Thank you.

Maria eyes her own engagement ring as she rubs the feet. The jewels sparkle even in the dim television glow.

Susan talks in a drowsy voice, as if to herself. My whole life has been a lie, Consuela. I've been a fool. I mean, I think all I ever truly wanted was a goofy husband, a house in the burbs, a yard, a couple of kids, a big old slobbery dog like Beethoven. Just like my own mother. I could have gone down that path. I had the chance. But I chose all of this instead. I chose the—what is it my mother called it—the unconventional path. Or did I just choose Meryl? I mean, did one odd encounter at an MLA convention, one night of wanton abandon, send me down this path? Do any of us ever really choose our path? Or is it all random dumb luck?

I don't know, Miss Susan.

Maria is thinking about Khalil—how he has said more than once that he wants to have three kids. He's imagined them already—described them to her in the dark, his face just a shape and a shadow. Second-generation mutts, is how he put it—preternaturally gifted imps with skin the color of burnished leather, hair the color of spun gold. (What if they come out stupid or unattractive? What if they come out stringy-haired rotten brats—with kinks of the soul, rather than kinks of the hair?)

They've talked about names. Khalil likes Thelonious, Joaquin, or Cheo for a boy. And Tuesday, Indigo, or Quincy for a girl. Names as predictable for the culturally elite mulatto spawn as June and May are for the Chinese adoptee, as Elijah is for the black adoptee. As unsurprising as Jasmine and Tiffany are for the working-class biracial girl of the white mother on food stamps.

She and Khalil have already agreed they will hyphenate their names after they get married. The children will be hyphenated too.

Indigo Mirsky-Pierce. Cheo Pierce-Mirsky.

Maria thinks how scripted it all feels. Even the wedding itself, down to the caterer they have chosen—a dandy from Harlem who takes his catering business to Martha's Vineyard—Oak Bluffs! The Inkwell!—every summer. He specializes in nouveau soul food—low-fat fried chicken, lard-free collard greens, low-sodium black-eyed peas, minus the bacon. Maria has heard Gloria's voice in her head: Um, hate to say this, but without the diabetes-inducing ingredients, it's not soul food.

Susan—at the other end of the couch, at the other end of the foot—is crying. We meet in all these strange hotels,

Consuela, and we screw and screw again and he makes me feel like I'm the only woman alive. But then he always goes back to Montclair, to that cow and those horrid utterly uninteresting children, and nothing ever changes. Tomorrow is Sunday and he will spend the day with them, doing what these people do, trudging around a mall or something, and I will be here, alone with June, in our cool, hip apartment, losing my bloody mind.

On-screen, the toddler has fallen into the swimming pool and is starting to sink beneath the surface. In slow motion, the dog, Beethoven, leaps in to save her.

Consuela?

Yes, Miss Susan?

He's never going to leave her, is he?

I don't believe he is.

Thank you for your honesty, Consuela. Thank you for that. I can always count on you to tell me the truth, Consuela. I appreciate that—you're no bullshit. She sighs. Christ, I need a drink. Vermouth on ice, please. It's on the counter.

Maria rises and goes to the kitchen, begins to fix Susan her drink.

I'm so tired, Consuela. I'm so tired of living in this city, in this apartment. Do you know I've been here, in this exact apartment, since I was twenty-eight? He's been my lover for that long. It used to be enough. But now I'm tired of being on my own. Especially now that I have June. I mean, I want somebody to share her with, to share in all those special moments. You know what I mean? I want that.

Maria has wanted it too—to play grown-up. And now she is getting it. The wedding dress. The ring. The house they will someday buy—not like the one in *Beethoven* exactly—not the hideous furniture and frumpy clothes and mushroom hairdos of the early-nineties-era white family in the movie. Theirs will be a brownstone in Brooklyn, filled with elegant natural wood finishes and indigo mud cloth pillows and authentic Lorna Simpson paintings gifted to them at their wedding. They will have dinner parties where they will serve jambalaya and all the guests will be witty and shining in shea butter. They will make adulthood look fun. So fun she will never know it happened. Their first baby will be like the messiah of Mulatto Nation. Mulatto-squared. M to the 2. Cheo Thelonious Mirsky-Pierce. What a mouthful.

By the time Maria brought Khalil home to meet Gloria—over spring break of senior year—the furor about the racist answering machine message had quelled on campus. The protesters had gone back to their schoolwork, realized they were paying a whole lot of tuition and would need to get jobs someday soon. Khalil was left with a box of surplus Audre Lorde T-shirts. He brought one for Gloria as a gift. She was impressed and immediately put it on.

She was already thin by then. The T-shirt hung from her skeletal frame like a dress.

She laid out the containers of Chinese takeout she'd ordered while Khalil told her about his globe-trotting upbringing. They were still in the middle of the conversation, and of dinner, when Khalil fell asleep. He just nodded off while sitting in front of his half-eaten food. He sat like a puppet at the table, his head lolling forward slightly, his smile still frozen on his lips so that he looked not so much asleep as like a drunken blind man.

I think he has narcolepsy, Maria said to Gloria as she chewed a piece of fried tofu.

Oh well, Gloria said. Nobody's perfect. You should still marry him. Like, tomorrow.

Maria stood up to clear the dishes. I don't know, Gloria. I mean, we're so young. We're only in college.

So what? College, schmollege. Don't be an idiot. All your life you've wanted to know if you could be everything at once. You've wanted to have it all. You were always such a having girl. Well, here's your chance, kid. Somebody heard your prayers. Because narcolepsy or not, he's all that you ever wanted and more than you'll need. Trust me on this one.

You don't think we're too young to decide on a mate?

Gloria sighed. The biggest, stupidest cultural shift to ever happen in my lifetime was when people stopped marrying their college boyfriend or girlfriend. When they decided they had to fuck and "try out" a whole panoply of bodies after college. That they had to do all these fake marriages before the real one. I mean, Jesus, I should have married Frank Delroy, trust me on this one. I shouldn't have waited until I was stuck with H and all his phallocentric bullshit.

But you always say you were on a journey, Gloria.

Fuck that. You go on a journey whether you're married or not. I mean, you think meeting "the one" gets easier as you get older and more bitter with each passing year? It isn't easier. You just get more fucking rigid and one day you wake up and you're forty-five and perimenopausal and going on a cruise to Alaska with your best girlfriend. You don't get that many chances to be happy. And any stretch of happiness, by the way, only ever lasts two weeks. That's another rule you learn the hard way.

Maria hovered over the dinner table beside Gloria, her arms folded, watching Khalil's sleeping face.

I don't know. Sometimes it feels too easy.

Easy? Oh Jesus. Listen to me. I'm your mother, or at least acting like I'm your mother. They aren't going to let me stay in this graduate student housing much longer. They have a twenty-year limit on that shit or something. Any way, you're going to need a home of your own. Gloria shook her head. You would be a stone-cold idiot not to marry this guy. Shit. I didn't even know they made this model of guy. Look at this T-shirt he brought me.

She pulled her shirt taut and stared at the master's house quote upside down. A man who loves Audre Lorde. If that's not enough to wet your panties—

That was my idea, Maria said. I told him to make the T-shirts after the, you know, racial incident. I introduced him to Audre Lorde.

So what? He agreed to it. He signed his name to it. He sent the template to the T-shirt factory, didn't he?

Gloria picked up Khalil's wineglass across the table and swallowed what was left in it. She gave Maria a sidelong glance. Listen, the point is, you should marry him. Right quick. I mean, if this cat got any more perfect for you, he'd be—you.

Maria began to gather their plates, loudly, trying to wake Khalil up. He didn't flinch. He sat there, head lolling forward, the smile still on his lips, like a beautiful, golden, life-sized man doll.

Gloria watched him. I think the narcolepsy is adorable. Someday you'll be happy for these little lulls. Who the fuck wants a man to be awake all the time?

■ ■ ■

Maria brings Susan her glass of vermouth. Susan takes the glass but glimpses Maria's hand before she can pull it away.

Wait a minute, Susan says, grabbing Maria's hand and turning it this way and that, examining the stones on her ring.

Did Ricky finally propose?

Yes.

Oh, Consuela. That's fabulous. And this looks almost real. God. They've gotten so good. It's fabulous.

Maria tries to pull her hand away but Susan holds tight, her eyes fixed on the ring.

Where'd he get this, anyway? Susan says.

He wouldn't tell me.

Susan squints at it. Well, it looks real. Make sure nobody chops your finger off for it. She releases Maria's hand and takes a gulp from the glass, smacks her lips. Good for Ricky. Two kids later, he finally got it together.

I have to go home now, Miss Susan.

I know. I know you have to go home. The money is all there. Including last week's. You can count it. Susan nods toward a wad of cash on the table.

Thank you, Miss Susan. She eyes the money, but doesn't take it. She knows it makes no sense, but she has the feeling that if she takes the money, she will be acknowledging that she's been here. If she leaves it there, on the table, it will all have been a dream.

What time can I expect you on Monday?

Monday. Monday. Distantly, Maria remembers the other world. On Monday Maria is supposed to be a highly educated quadroon named Maria set to be married to a highly educated mulatto named Khalil. Monday she is supposed to go to the library to work on her dissertation about Jonestown. Monday, no more Consuela.

She goes to stand by the window. She presses her forehead against the cold glass. It is snowing outside now. Large, cartoon-like flakes drift down before the window and Maria thinks about the snow globe in the poet's apartment. She imagines she is tiny and has ended up inside that snow globe. She turns her head so that her cheek rests flat on the glass. She's trying to see his window from here, but from this angle she can't quite make it out.

It is clearly time to tell Susan the truth. As soon as she tells her, it will be over. She will not be buzzed inside the building again. She may never get this close to the poet's apartment again. She may never again have the chance to lie in his bed and hold his pillow to her face and breathe in his wholesome scent.

Gloria. Gloria. Gloria. If she were alive today, what would she tell her to do? Gloria had a dozen bumper stickers on her car. *Feminism is to womanism as lavender is to purple. A woman needs a man like a fish needs a bicycle. Well-behaved women seldom make history. Sisterhood is powerful!* Her car was like an anthology on wheels. *This Bridge Called My Car.* She made Maria watch *Roots* every year it came on and bought her a subscription to *Essence* when she turned fourteen. She always wanted her to become the daughter she'd been dreaming about, the sweetest of dark berries. And she never did.

Gloria always told Maria to tell the truth. She said, The consequences of the truth are never as bad as the lie. But would Gloria love her now, if she knew all her secrets?

Something comes back to Maria now. It flickers before her eyes like a crackling old film reel. The time she went to a roller disco with Gloria. She must have been eight. The disco was called Spin Off—a converted loft in a building in Back Bay. You had to climb three flights of spiral stairs to get there.

Maria whizzed in circles to Sylvester's "You Make Me Feel Mighty Real" while Gloria sat somewhere on the sidelines reading *Dust Tracks on a Road* for the umpteenth time, highlighter pen perched over the text.

Later, while Gloria went downstairs to get the car to pull it around, Maria sat upstairs in the fourth-floor lobby just a few feet away from the spiral staircase, changing out of her roller skates and into her sneakers. When she looked up from her sneakers she saw that one of her roller skates was rolling away, all by itself, to the edge of the landing. Maria was mesmerized by the sight of her roller skate moving alone, away from its pair, as if pushed by an invisible hand. She sat, frozen, as it rolled to the edge of the landing and then disappeared over the edge. A second of horrible silence, then a thud and shout. Shrieks. She rose and walked to the bannister. Her skate had landed three flights below on a girl's head. She could see the girl lying on the floor, her hair spread around her face. She was either knocked out or dead, Maria couldn't say which.

Maria's other roller skate sat behind her by the bench, as

if it had wickedly pushed its twin toward the edge. Her heart wild with fear, she picked it up and held it as she headed down the stairs to meet her fate.

She could hear someone—maybe the girl's mother—shouting and crying, I'll kill the motherfucker that did this to my baby.

Maria's eyes stung as she imagined her funeral. She got to the bottom of the stairs and there, a small huddle of people stood over the girl, who was not in fact dead, but was just sitting up, rubbing her head and moaning. Several employees of the roller disco were racing around trying to assuage the family and looking out the door to see if the ambulance had arrived.

Maria glimpsed, at the edge of the crowd, her other roller skate lying on its side, the twin of the one she held in her hand. It was so obvious that she was the culprit, to anybody who decided to look. A nervous, shifty-eyed girl clutching one roller skate—with a pink pom-pom on the back just like the one that had fallen. If that wasn't a smoking gun. She picked up the errant skate, then turned to face the group, ready to accept the blame. The eyes of the girl's mother rolled over Maria, then slid past her, searching for somebody, it seemed, behind her.

I swear, the mother kept saying, I'll kill the motherfucker.

There was a familiar beeping outside. Maria stood there, waiting for another beat, waiting to be seen, but people looked through her, past her, searching for the someone who had done it.

Maria put the pair of skates in her bag, zipped it shut, and walked slowly outside, where Gloria's Pacer was idling at the curb.

Gloria sat in the front seat smoking, listening to music with the window open.

What happened in there? Gloria said, staring out at the ambulance that had just pulled up. Two EMTs rushed out and into the building.

A girl got hurt, Maria said, staring out the window at the neon sign, Spin Off. The first three letters were burned out so that it read, simply, N OFF.

■ ■ ■

The snow is falling more heavily now. Maria catches her reflection in the glass. Somehow, her nose looks pointier than she remembers it, her features more elfin.

Susan, she says, I'm not the person you think I am. I'm not—well, I'm not Consuela. I didn't mean to mislead you. I would have told you but you were on the phone. You were upset. I didn't know what to do. I wanted to tell you the truth, but you were already gone when I came out. It wasn't my fault—it just kind of happened.

There. She has said it. She has told the truth. It feels good, just like Gloria always said it would.

I am sorry, Maria says, her chin tilted up at what she thinks is a dignified angle. I didn't mean any harm.

She waits for Susan's response—rage or pity, anything, she's ready—but it doesn't come. There is only silence.

When she turns around, she sees Susan is asleep. Her mouth hangs open. The glass of vermouth rests on her chest, her hand loosely wrapped around it. On the screen, the movie is over. Some pop rendition of Chuck Berry's "Roll Over Beethoven" plays over the credits.

They are all there, seated together at the back of the restaurant, beneath a million blinking chili-pepper lights.

Lisa is wearing a plum-colored head wrap. She sits at the end of the table, looking regal, luminous, her eyebrows perfectly coy arches. The head wrap is working for her tonight, Maria thinks. It no longer looks like she's hiding something. It no longer looks kitchen-worker chic. Context is everything. It's true she is still a pastry chef in training at that Soho bakery, learning to make increasingly intricate French pastries, but she is considering applying to art school. She is considering a career as a painter. She talked about it the last time they were together. She'd taken some quiz in a career counselor's office that showed she was a visual-spatial learner. Maria feels now an almost big-sisterly pride as she stands on the other side of the glass, watching Lisa hold court.

Maria can see Khalil too, his dreadlocks piled in an enormous bun on top of his head, sitting hunched over a plate of Bangladeshi food, eating with his fingers.

Gloria used to say to her: You can't have it all. If you're a black woman in America, you have to choose which thing you will get. For a long time Maria took everything Gloria said to be God-given fact, but now she thinks Gloria was wrong.

The last time she'd gone with Khalil to visit his parents in Seattle, his father, Sam, set up a projector in the living room. After dinner they all sat down to watch a slide show of photographs from the Mirskys' travels. Maria sat between Khalil and Lisa on the couch, watching the images move past. She had seen some of their pictures before, and they'd always filled her with suspicion. She had never been able to see them without imagining Gloria there too, seated in the corner on an African Senufo stool, watching them all in uneasy silence.

But on that last visit, she'd felt herself relax into the Mirskys' story—to become part of it for the very first time. She laughed at their stories as if they were her stories too. There was Lisa, small and sun-burnished, standing in a dusty Senegalese village; there was Sam, frolicking, shirtless, in Costa Rican waves; there was Diane, weaving baskets with Bushwomen in Zimbabwe; and Khalil, at thirteen, playing chess with local teenagers in a village square in Mumbai.

Maria stares at them now through the restaurant glass. If she blurs her eyes just right, the scene looks magical, like another America she has been traveling toward all her life. Her breath makes fog on the glass as she peers inside.

Then, by and by, a revelation prickles to life inside of her. There is a figure at the end of the table she did not notice before. She wipes at the glass with her mittened hand, trying to see beyond the fog circles she's made. Her eyes sting and water. It is a figure she didn't notice at first. A one-of-these-things-is-not-like-the-other. A figure she recognizes.

She heads through the jingling door and stands inside the warmth of the restaurant, not breathing. She is filled with mirth. She almost laughs aloud. It is him. It is the poet. Alive and well. He has somehow, without her noticing, moved from the periphery, a casual acquaintance whose readings they have attended, whose work they have admired, to the inner circle. He is one of the eight people who have come to celebrate Lisa's twenty-fifth birthday. Everything seems to go silent around her as she stands there thawing, the snow turning into wetness on her shoulders, her skin tingling to life.

Ma'am? Ma'am?

The restaurant host—a haughty man in a blue blazer—is speaking to her.

Ma'am? he says. You're dripping all over the floor.

She looks at her feet and sees the puddle forming. I'm melting, she says, with a laugh.

The host doesn't smile. The bathrooms are for customers only, he says.

I am a customer. I'm with that table over there. She points behind him at the table—at the poet, yes, the poet.

That's my party, she says. Just over there.

When she gets to the table, Lisa rises to give her a hug.

Maria takes a furtive glance at the poet over Lisa's shoulder. He is not looking in her direction, but it's him. He is really here.

They pull apart and Lisa spots the bag twisted around Maria's hand. She smiles, touches her chest. For li'l old me?

Maria remembers that she was supposed to bring Lisa a birthday present. Something special from her and Khalil. She hands Lisa the plastic record shop bag and says, Happy birthday.

Lisa, grinning, pulls out the old Stacy Lattisaw album. She stares at the sleeve with a confused smile. Oh. What's this?

An album. You remember that song, "Love on a Two-Way Street."

As soon as she says it, she realizes Lisa would not remember this song. Maria has nearly forgotten that Lisa was not always a Negro. While Maria was listening to Patrice Rushen and Stacy Lattisaw alone in her pantry-sized bedroom, Lisa was living somewhere off the grid, in Mumbai or Calcutta. And later, when she got back to the United States, she did not become the kind of girl to listen to Stacy Lattisaw. Maria has been inside Lisa's teenaged bedroom in Seattle, has seen the yellowing concert flyer for the Violent Femmes on her corkboard.

Lisa holds the Stacy Lattisaw album as if it is a bag of flaming dung Maria has handed her. Her eyes flash with anger. This is the big surprise? she says to Khalil. Then, in a mocking tone, You guys shouldn't have.

Khalil leans over to Maria. I thought you were picking up the doll, he whispers.

She stares at him blankly for a moment. The doll. Then it comes back to her. She isn't sure how she could have forgotten. It is a doll they ordered months ago for this very occasion—made by a woman in Harlem, a modern-day folk artist who goes by the name Ceres Dalton. Dolls for adults, by Ceres.

It goes like this: You give Ceres a photograph of a person you want made into a doll, and in a few months, voilà, she makes it. She sculpts the faces out of resin. The bodies are made of cloth stuffed with cotton batting, soft but with just enough weight in the bottom that you can prop them up on a piano or a bookshelf and they will sit there, watching you. Khalil saw her work listed in a magazine—a Doll by Ceres is one of the top ten gifts to give this year.

Khalil and Maria went up to the woman's studio one afternoon a few months ago with a photograph of Lisa laughing in a head wrap. They paid the deposit. Maria thought it was all a scam, just like the woman herself was a scam.

While they were there, Maria pointed out to Khalil that the sample dolls Ceres showed them all had the same face, the same puckish features, only the skin tones and outfits were different. They all looked like the doll-maker, Ceres, who looked like she was made out of resin herself, her skin flawless, her curls crisp and unmoving.

The doll had been scheduled to be picked up this week. Khalil has planned it all so meticulously to make his sister's birthday feel special. The studio isn't far from the university library where Maria works each day. It was all to be so easy—an easy task she has failed to do. And scam or no scam, what a great feat that would have been, to pass the doll dressed as Lisa around at this dinner table to oohs and aahs. Lisa would be smiling at her and Khalil lovingly, rather than wearing a disappointed grimace as she tries to find a place to hide the old Stacy Lattisaw record on the floor behind her chair.

The poet. He is here. It is almost too much that he is here, so close to her, after all that has happened today. She sits straight-backed in her chair for a count of twenty before she allows herself to turn and look at him. He's eating his Bangladeshi food with a fork. He catches her eye and lifts his glass of beer.

Stacy Lattisaw, he says. Nice one.

Electricity moves through her. She smiles, blushes, nods, tries to think of something clever to say back, but can't. She is without words. He likes the music she picked out. He alone understands the true genius of the gift she gave Lisa. Of course. If they were alone they would listen to the album together. And she knows that she has to get the album back from Lisa somehow. She will tell Lisa it was a joke. That she was only kidding when she gave her the worst birthday present in the world. She will explain later that there is a real gift, because there is a real gift, the doll that looks exactly like her—in a generic, all-mulattos-look-alike way. And Lisa will gladly give the album back to her, laughing, all forgiven.

She thinks of something to say to the poet. She will ask him if he's ever been to Paris. She will feel the frisson of knowing she has stood in his apartment shaking the snow globe with the Eiffel Tower inside.

But before she can say it, he's already turned his attention away. He's talking to somebody else—a girl at his side. Maria feels a prickle of discomfort. The girl has red hair and freckles and a big silly smile. Her strange pointy breasts jut out under a tight green sweater, torpedo tits out of an old *Gidget* movie. In college, Claudette used to call boobs like that "sweater meat."

Could this bizarre creature be his date—the one he talked to on the phone before leaving his apartment? Could this possibly be his type?

The girl leans in and says something to him. Her mouth is a little too close to his ear. They laugh and nod together. Maria feels sick. She thinks she might actually get sick. She picks up a piece of naan from the center of the table and takes several bites, filling her mouth completely with the bread, realizing only now that she is starving. She has not eaten since the hot dog in the park. The naan has an odd smell. Dirty. She puts the bread down and touches her lips and realizes the smell is coming from her own fingers. She didn't wash her hands after giving Susan the foot massage. She stands and heads to the restroom, face blazing. There she washes her hands furiously with soap and hot water. She stares at herself in the mirror.

The Chinese baby—June—had looked so alarmed when she leaned over her crib. She had looked at Maria with such suspicion, almost hatred, until the very end.

Maria hears a sigh from the toilets behind her. She thought she was alone in here, but she is not. She turns to look at the closed stall door. She is about to crouch down to see what kind of shoes they are wearing when the restroom door swings open and Lisa steps inside.

She stands beside Maria at the sink, teasing her hair, reapplying her lipstick. She's oddly quiet.

You okay? Maria asks.

Lisa doesn't answer.

You look pretty tonight, Maria says.

Lisa glances at her, then away, as if bored by the banal compliment. She hands Maria a tube of lipstick. Here, she says, you need some color.

Maria takes the lipstick, but can't help being distracted by the person in the stall. Why aren't there sounds of defecation? Urination? What are they doing? What is taking them so long? She applies the lipstick and sees it does make her look better. She thinks about the poet and dabs some of the lipstick on her cheeks, rubs it in like rouge. That red-haired girl can't be his type.

She knows this much: She needs to find out. She tries to sound casual.

So, she says to Lisa: Who invited Raggedy Anne?

Excuse me?

Maria shrugs. You know, the girl with the freckle face.

You mean Shura?

If you must. Shura. Okay. Shura. Maria laughs.

Lisa doesn't laugh. She just shakes her head. Unbelievable, she says.

What's unbelievable?

You are.

How's that?

Lisa's lips are thin. Well, for starters, you show up nearly an hour late for Oma at the bridal salon wearing that sticker. I mean, she's eighty-two years old. Was that really necessary? Then you show up late for my birthday, dressed like, like, I don't know what. Like you forgot. And, I'm sorry—that gift? You're about to become my sister. And you didn't even spend any time trying to get me a gift that has any meaning. I felt like you just grabbed any old thing off the street.

I can explain that, Maria says. There's a story behind that gift. And, I don't want to ruin the surprise, but there's another gift coming, and you will not be—

Lisa cuts her off. And now you decide to insult my friend. I grew up with Shura. Did you know that? We went to the same Montessori. And you know what else? She just recovered from a serious bacterial illness. She could have died. I invited her because she's one of my oldest and dearest friends and she wanted to come out tonight to enjoy herself after everything she's been through.

She almost died? She doesn't look like it.

What is that supposed to mean?

Nothing. I just. Maria hangs her head. She shrugs. I'm sorry about everything.

Is everything a joke to you, Maria? Lisa shakes her head and starts to talk about how she already considers Maria family and how it's a big deal that Maria is about to become one of the Mirskys—and how much they all love her

and care about her and that's what this is all about, really—
wanting to be sure she understands that.

There is something going on inside the stall behind
them. Somebody is shifting positions, sighing in there.
Maria bends down to peek under the stall but she can't see
any shoes at all. Which means that the person either has
no feet or that they are crouching on the toilet seat, eaves-
dropping.

Are you even listening to me? Lisa says.

Of course I am.

Because you seem like your mind is elsewhere.

Maria turns back to Lisa. No, no. I'm here.

Are you? I don't know what the hell is going on with
you, Maria, but pull it together. Pull it to-fucking-gether.

Maria has more to say—she wants to explain about the
gift that is coming—she is prepared to ruin the surprise and
say it: a Lisa Doll by Ceres Dalton. But she doesn't get to
say it, because Lisa is gone, sweeping out of the bathroom,
leaving Maria in the stillness.

It is very quiet now. Maria turns back to look at the stall
door. She clears her throat.

Who's in there? she says.

Nobody answers.

Why are you just—hanging out in there?

There is no answer.

Who are you?

Silence.

She steps forward, adrenaline pumping, touches the door lightly, and it swings open. The stall is empty.

■ ■ ■

They are already singing "Happy Birthday" when she gets back to the table. The cake is a work of high art—a sublime golden confection, created especially for Lisa by her friends at the bakery. Maria slides in beside Khalil, mouthing the words, her eyes now fixed on the redhead, Shura, who sings hardest and loudest of all. Maria feels a little better now that she knows the girl came alone. And if she really did just make it through a medical calamity, this means that she was probably not fooling around with boys. Still, she is sitting too close to the poet and keeps flashing goofy smiles at him while she sings along.

Khalil puts a hand on Maria's knee. Everything all right?

She picks up a wineglass and gulps what's left in it. I think your sister hates me.

She doesn't hate you.

I'm sorry about the doll.

Hey. Look at me.

What?

It's okay. I forgive you. And you know what else?

What's that?

I love you.

He tugs her chin toward him. He begins to kiss her soft and slow on the lips. She can feel Lisa's eyes on them, and she returns the kiss as best she can, thinking, Either I'm wooden or he's wooden—one of us is wooden.

She hears Lisa say, You two are killing me. Go get a room.

Maria kisses him back, but her mind is on the poet, and the horrifying possibility that he is watching them go at it. She pulls abruptly away, wipes her lips, and looks over at him.

To her relief, he hasn't seen a thing. He's too busy eating his slice of birthday cake with full concentration. He savors small bites like a child. She thinks it is perhaps the most beautiful thing she has ever seen, the poet enjoying his slice of cake. And as if he can hear her thoughts, he glances up from his work of eating and catches her eye. She doesn't smile and he doesn't either. They watch each other across the table beneath the chili-pepper lights and she thinks he looks a little unsettled by what is passing between them. He frowns and looks down at his cake, then up at her again, chewing what is left in his mouth slowly before swallowing.

■ ■ ■

It is almost midnight when they all stand up to leave.

The poet and Khalil and Lisa and the rest of them grab coats and mittens and with drunken laughter extract themselves from the table, head toward the door. Maria lingers at the table, fiddling with her bag. She has spotted something on the seat where the poet was sitting. She needs to investigate. When the others are outside, she picks it up with trembling hands. It is a hat. A knit cap. It is his cap. It has to be his, a man's knit Pittsburgh Steelers cap. The blood rushes into her ears. She shoves the cap into her purse and zips it shut.

Outside, a waiter is standing, coatless, shivering, waiting for them to assemble so he can take their photograph.

Hurry up, slowpoke! Lisa shouts.

Another voice—a slim mulatto girl she has never seen before tonight—says, Homegirl's slowing around! Maria smirks at the poet, wondering if he too can see how forced it all is—this group and the pantomime of their newly discovered blackness. It's catching. The craze. We once were lost, but now we're black. It's so old-school it's new-school. They have taken on their duties as Negroes with aplomb, she's gotta give them that. They are born-again black people. They weeble and wobble on their new roller skates and almost fall, but she has to give them an A for effort.

Maria joins the group. On one side of her stands Khalil, on the other is Shura, who puts her arm around Maria and pulls her in close as if they are old friends. The waiter steps back with the camera and says, Ready?

Khalil shouts, Everyone repeat after me: Bada bye bye.

He says the words in a Jamaican accent like they do in

the reggae songs. And everybody repeats after Khalil. Bada bye bye! they cry, just as the light flashes, blinding them momentarily.

■ ■ ■

Maria and Khalil have sex that night on the floor of their apartment. Maria makes soft moaning sounds and moves her hips around, but she can't lose herself. When she closes her eyes, she envisions two chairs slamming together, wood cracking, finally breaking apart until they are a pile of parts on the floor. He is still inside her. She tries to imagine a basic image: two white people fucking. The woman has big tits and a tiny waist; a man has a dully handsome Ken doll face and a flat stomach. This isn't the first time she's seen them. As an adolescent, she used to sketch this pair in her diary, this crude sketch of naked Caucasoid people fucking, like the first cave-drawing porn. She would stare at the sketch while she listened to Michael Jackson's "She's Out of My Life." She doesn't know who the people in the image are—she has never met anyone like them in real life. She herself is nowhere to be found in the image she conjures. She just imagines the white couple in different positions and eventually grows aroused. She comes in a mechanical way and Khalil comes a few moments later, then collapses on top of her. She wonders but doesn't ask what kind of bodies he has imagined behind his eyes.

Greg came by her dorm room unannounced one afternoon a month after their breakup. He said he was there to retrieve his father's old Connecticut College sweatshirt. As she fished it out of her closet, he said to her: I see you have a new boyfriend.

At the time, she knew whom he was talking about. Greg must have spotted her somewhere on campus, holding hands with the new guy. He wasn't exactly a boyfriend. His name was Trent Cook and he was a proud member of Alpha Phi Alpha fraternity and a stiff closet case. She had never so much as kissed Trent. He came from a political family in

Washington, DC, and wanted to run for mayor someday. He had told her when they first met that she looked like Effi Barry. She didn't know how to take it, but everybody in Ujamaa said they were a cute couple and she felt a frisson of pleasure at the sight of their reflection walking together, hand in hand, across campus. She looked like a different person beside him—a well-heeled girl who had grown up in DC and attended Jack and Jill and was now thinking of pledging AKA.

Even her features looked different beside Trent, less random, more Talented Tenth. Strangers all her life thought Maria was from somewhere else—Iraq, Israel, Mexico— but beside him, she looked as American as Ida B. Wells. She admired the way she looked on Trent's arm. It was too bad for her that Trent was, as Gloria would say, gay as the day is long.

So is it serious? Greg said to her now. He was pretending not to care.

Not really, she said, thinking of how Trent always held his hips and butt a mile away when they hugged, as if her vagina might bite him if he got too close. He'd told her the night before last that her nose was awfully large; he asked her if she'd ever considered rhinoplasty, then quickly said he was only kidding.

Maria placed the sweatshirt on her bed. Greg stared at it but didn't move to pick it up.

Tell me something, Maria, he said. Where did you learn to be so cold?

I learned from my masters, she said back in her best impression of Olivia de Havilland. She smiled, trying to keep things light. Did you ever see that movie? What was it called?

I'm serious, Greg said, wearing a pained expression. How did you get to be like this? I'm curious.

Like what?

You're a monster, Greg said, flatly.

Maria went and stood by the window. The campus was coated in the too pretty light of late afternoon. A pack of pin-thin, ponytailed girls jogged past her dormitory. In the distant field she could see a boy had attached a thick rope between two trees and was practicing tightrope-walking across it. He kept falling off midway across and then climbing back on to try again.

She once thought there was nothing more beautiful than that campus. The first time she visited, she had thought, I could die here. But standing there just then, she actually felt dead inside, which was a different thing altogether. She missed the steel gray light of the other coast, the winter-hardened faces of her neighbors, the cramped graduate student housing she called home. She missed her mother fiercely, the mother who had gone half-mad trying to finish the longest dissertation in the history of the world. She thought about how everybody misses their mother when they are dying—even the most hardened soldiers on the battlefield called out for mama just before they took their last breath. When she was a child, she'd had severe separation anxiety. Whenever Gloria would drop her off at school, she'd cling to her leg, drag along the ground after her, screaming: Don't go. It lasted all the way through second grade. When her mother brought her to a child psychologist, the therapist said it wasn't separation anxiety—it was attachment anxiety. It meant Maria wasn't properly attached. That was why Maria couldn't stand to be apart from her mother. She was not confident in their attachment.

The therapist said it was typical of adopted children. The therapist had no good ideas of how to fix it—just the right words to make her mother feel exactly worthless.

Gloria left the meeting distraught. Attachment anxiety? Are we not attached? she kept saying on the car ride home.

But Maria thought the therapist had been wrong. There was no difference between separation anxiety and attachment anxiety—they were the very same thing.

She could feel Greg's eyes boring into her back. The sweatshirt he'd come to retrieve lay on the bed, waiting to be claimed. It was possible she was his first truly bad experience.

She heard his voice behind her. Were you molested as a child, Maria?

She turned to look at him. Seriously?

Yeah. Seriously. I've wondered it before about you. I'm taking a psych class. You fit the description.

She felt a ticking in her brain.

Wait a minute, she said. Let me get this straight. I have to be damaged goods—molested—not to want to be with a white man.

That's not what I said. You're twisting my words again. Forget it.

But she was just getting started.

So it's unfathomable to you, she said pacing the small room now, that a person would choose to be black if given the option. You have this narrative implanted in your brain and you don't even know it. Progress equals whiteness. The closer we get to worshipping whiteness, fellating the giant white penis, the closer we are to sanity.

Jesus. Here we go again.

Was I molested? No, I wasn't fucking molested. I mean, no more than the average female born circa 1970. There was a plumber who watched me shower that one time when I was eleven. There was the homeless guy who jacked off in the movie theater while me and my best friend watched *Watership Down*. And there was the girl who pulled me into a closet that time and felt me up while bullying me. But none of it was worth mentioning ever because all of it was so banal and run of the mill. I mean, who hasn't been molested? That's the unusual thing. People who have never been molested.

I was just asking.

And no, just because I don't want to be with you doesn't mean I'm a psycho case. I find whiteness tiresome. Not even upsetting, really. Just boring—like a lecture you wish would end but keeps droning on and on and on for eternity.

Will you cut it out? he said. This isn't a tribunal. I'm not an Afrikaaner. I didn't enslave you or your people.

Oh yes you are, and yes you did.

She wasn't sure what she meant exactly by this part, but she let the words hang there, above them, glittery with rage.

I forgot how predictable you are, Maria. Thanks for reminding me.

No, you're predictable. I've seen this movie before. I remember how it ends. The white guy saves the world from imminent destruction. But not before his black best friend, the funny, dickless one, dies in a hail of gunfire. And not before the mulatto chick throws herself off a bridge. Yadda yadda yadda.

Just forget it. Just forget I ever gave a shit about you. You win. I'm a racist and an idiot and I'm sorry I ever burdened you with my existence. Excuse me. I'm going to kill myself now.

With that, he slammed out the door and was gone. He left his Connecticut College sweatshirt lying on her bed.

She didn't see Greg again for the rest of the year. He vanished. She worried about him and even thought to ask a boy from his dorm if he was still alive. The boy said he was.

He said Greg was lying low, spending a lot of time off campus, doing volunteer tutoring in East Palo Alto.

Summer came and she went back east and got a job working as an assistant to an acupuncturist in Newton. Gloria hooked her up with the job. Doctor Wang was a friend of Gloria's—they'd met at a yoga retreat in the Berkshires. Since that weekend, Gloria had officially quit all Western medicine. She only saw Doctor Wang and the homeopath, Chuck Whittle.

Doctor Wang hired Maria as her assistant that summer. She needed someone to help around her office, filing and tidying up; she told Maria she might even get to pull some needles out of patients if she was lucky.

Doctor Wang spoke only broken English. From the first day she gave Maria a white coat to wear, just like her own. That same day—after only the most rudimentary, ten-minute, mostly mimed training session—Doctor Wang allowed Maria to perform moxibustion, a procedure where she held a burning stick to a patient's skin. Closer, closer, Doctor Wang said—until the patient's flesh turned red and blistered. As the summer went on, she gave Maria more and more responsibilities. She gave her a list of patients with a time scrawled next to their names. Maria had to go in at that time and pull the needles out of their bodies. They were usually naked. She was nervous at first. In her youth she found the signs of decay, fat, wrinkles, and scars on the bodies of older adults disturbing. Her hands often trembled as she moved to pull the needles out. But over the summer she grew more adept. The bodies became just bodies. She pulled the longest needles she'd ever seen out of a woman's enormous pale ass. She pulled the most needles she'd ever seen at once out of a man's genital area, where they'd been arranged in his strawberry blond pubic hair in a kind of crop circle around his penis. Though Maria herself felt fine, Doctor Wang would ask her to stick out her tongue, and would feel her pulse and often sent her home with needles behind her ears or in her scalp, saying she thought Maria's energy was off. She was trying to balance Maria's energy.

When Maria returned to campus in the fall she saw what Greg had meant by "I'm going to kill myself now."

Because Greg Winnicott was dead, in a way.

She almost didn't recognize who he had become. His skin was darker—a strange shiny reddish brown, as if coated in a layer of shellac. He wore a thin ponytail down his neck that seemed too long to have grown in after only a few months. He was wearing short-shorts that seemed too tight for his now thick thighs, and a tight blue tank top with an iron-on image of a rainbow across his chest.

Maria stood watching him from the shadows of an oak tree, wanting to look away but somehow unable. He was shouting orders to the group of Latino high school kids who wore bright prison-orange T-shirts with the name of an after-school mentorship club across the back. He spoke in a Latino inflection, peppering his sentence with Spanish words as if he were searching but failing to find the English equivalent.

The painting they were doing was only half finished but she got the idea: Aztec faces turned up to the sky, fists raised, an Indio mother, squat and sturdy with cherubic baby strapped to her back. When it was finished a few weeks later, they'd given text to the image. It said, *Monocultures Die Out.*

It has been six days since Maria last saw the poet. She still has his hat in her possession. She wears it sometimes, just locally, to go to the store to buy milk, or in the privacy of her apartment, reading over the files at her desk.

At first she was trying to put it on only when Khalil was out, but a few days ago he came home early and found her wearing it while she fixed them dinner.

Where'd you get that hat? Have you been robbing homeless people again?

I bought it off the street, she said, touching it gently.

Let me try it on. He pulled it off her head. It's weirdly cool.

Maria snatched it from him and said, with a harshness that surprised her, It's mine, don't touch it. She tugged it back on her head and said in a calmer voice, It won't fit over your dreadlocks anyway.

The hat is nothing special. Just an ordinary knit cap. Eighty-five percent acrylic, fifteen percent wool. Machine wash cold, line dry. The Pittsburgh Steelers insignia has been ironed on. The poet comes from Pittsburgh. She somehow knows this detail about him. She smells the hat, fondles it, handles it often just to think of him. For the first few days after the party, there was a clear smell of his hair caught in the fibers—sweetness, strawberry and vanilla, undercut by something sharper and more male. Now, six days into this, the scent is almost gone. She has to press the fabric with increasing force against her nose, to inhale more deeply, just to get the slightest hint of what was so easily gotten before. And she knows that every day she holds it, wears it, rubs it on her skin, more of him is lost.

Today is the day she will call him. She promised herself she would give it a week. It has been six days—good enough. If she lets too much time pass, the energy that has passed between them over dinner will disappear. She has memorized his phone number. She has been waiting for this moment and preparing, walking around reciting the seven digits in her head as if they are a poem. She hears in their numerical pattern a kind of music. She has already dialed the number before, twice, in the evening. Each time his machine picked up. Each time she found the act of calling and not speaking to him satisfying in its own right. Each time she enjoyed the way his voice sounded on the answering machine, rushed and irritable and curious all at once. Each time she was almost relieved not to get him on the phone, because it prolonged the period when she had his hat in her possession.

She isn't sure he will answer this time, but she is ready to speak if he does. She is ready to use the only excuse she may ever have again to see him alone. I have your hat. I've been meaning to call. Let me know when we can meet up so I can give it back to you.

It is the perfect excuse, banal and unimpeachable. The luck of her being able to take the hat so easily that night, to shove it into her bag, seems like a miracle. She allows herself at times to wonder if he left it there for her on purpose, lying there on the seat, a beckoning of sorts, the way a girl in a cartoon drops a handkerchief.

Khalil has already gone to work. He left early to meet with Ethan and some investors in midtown about the start-up. It is mid-morning, the writing hour, when the poet will likely be at home. She puts on the hat so that it covers her eyes and stands in the middle of the living room holding the phone. She dials.

Jubilation. He answers on the second ring. Something

springs open within her at the sound of his real voice. Hello? His voice sounds creaky, almost prepubescent. She can hear the television in the background—a newscaster's flat accentless voice announcing that a tornado is about to hit the Midwest.

It is the moment, she realizes, when everything is about to change. The utterance of her name. She grips the phone tightly in her hand as she says, It's Maria. Maria Pierce.

He pauses. Oh, right. Maria. Hey, how are you?

She tells him she's fine. He says he's fine too. He asks her what she's up to. She says, Just chilling. She winces after she says it. She asks him what he's doing. He says he's writing, though she can still hear the television in the background.

Listen, she says, tugging the hat lower over her eyes. There's a reason I'm calling you.

She lets the words rest there. She wants his suspense to build.

Oh yeah?

I have something of yours. Something I know you'll want back.

What's that?

Your hat.

She has imagined this conversation in her head so many times and she expects him to say, Oh man, are you serious? Wow. I've been wondering about that hat. When can I get it back?

Instead, he says, What hat?

Your Pittsburgh Steelers hat.

Wait, did I leave it at Lisa's party?

Yeah. I grabbed it but didn't get a chance to give it to you then. I—meant to, but forgot.

Oh. Thanks.

I'd like to find a way to get it back to you. Is there somewhere we can meet? Maybe for a drink? I know the temperature is dropping this week. I'd hate to think of your head getting cold.

He is silent.

So just tell me where I can meet you and I'll bring it to you, okay?

Um, you don't have to go through the trouble. Honestly. I have other hats.

She pulls the hat so that it covers not only her eyes but also her nose and lips. She tries to control the feeling of panic that has washed over her.

No, she says, No. It's no trouble at all. I want to give it back to you. It's a great hat. And, see, I have this weird thing where I think it's important, always, to return things to their rightful owners. It's, like, an energetic thing. I can't explain it. So let's meet and I'll return it to you. Okay? Let's just meet for a drink and I'll give you the cap and you will have it back and you can do with it what you want.

She is pacing as she speaks, the wool over her mouth growing moist where her breath comes out.

Okay, he says. If it's like that, we can meet.

She feels the air in the room shift directions. He wants to meet. She pulls the hat off her head. The air of the room feels cold against her face. She feels naked without the hat over her eyes and mouth. In the mirror over the mantel, she can see her hair is wild with static, her skin mottled from the heat.

He says he can meet her in two days at a bar in the Village. He's going to be in that area around four. Can she meet him at four at this bar on West Fourth?

She can. Oh yes she can.

After they hang up, she stands, a little shocked, in the aftermath. Everything around her looks different. The scattered evidence of her life with Khalil already looks like vestiges: the Peter Tosh album propped up by the stereo, the Moosewood cookbook beside the stove, the Hanif Kureishi novel dog-eared on the sofa, the jar of coconut-scented dreadlock balm on the counter. There is the bulletin board over her desk across the room where so many months ago, on the advice of a magazine article, she tried to start a *dream board*—magazine tear-outs of glowing, caramel-skinned models getting married. In one image a couple is running, barefoot, teeth bared in ecstasy, on a white sand beach. In another, an equally caramel-skinned, equally ecstatic bride and groom are hand-feeding each other slices of wedding cake. Maria feels a tug of sadness—horror—at what she is about to do, but it passes. She has no time for regrets. There are only two days before she sees the poet.

She has work to do. She has only two days to improve everything about herself.

■　■　■

The next evening she stands in front of the full-length mirror, teasing her hair, trying to decide if it is good different or bad different. She has spent the bulk of the afternoon—what felt like a lifetime—in a beauty shop being groomed and coiffed, peeled and scrubbed. She hears Khalil opening the door to the apartment, his keys jingling, his voice calling, Maria! Then she hears the sound of a second voice. He is not alone. He has brought Ethan with him. She is surprised. Khalil rarely brings Ethan to their house. He usually goes to Ethan's apartment so as to avoid having to deal with the tension between him and Maria.

It's been this way between Maria and Ethan for a while. Since college, really. When Khalil discovered he was black, he dumped all his white friends from the Enchanted Broccoli Forest. Ethan is the only white friend who remains from those pre-Maria days—and now that he and Khalil are starting a business together, Maria knows Ethan is here to stay.

He makes her uncomfortable. It isn't just the way Khalil teases her in Ethan's presence—the incessant jokes about her being old-school, a Luddite, an Amish girl, or the way Ethan laughs a little too long at those jokes. The source of their tension goes back years, to when she and Ethan had a fight—a strangely vicious fight that seemed to come out of nowhere. They were both a little drunk. She said she didn't like Woody Allen movies and Ethan accused her of being anti-Semitic. She accused him of being racist. They ended up screaming accusations at each other on an East Village street while Khalil tried to calm them both down. They apologized to each other at a brunch Khalil organized for this purpose a few weeks later, but it was the kind of outburst you don't forget.

She comes to greet them in the dark hallway, where they stand removing hats and coats and boots. She switches on the light and Khalil does a double take at the sight of her new hair.

Wow, he says. Wow.

The salon she went to today was nothing fancy—a Jamaican storefront salon a few blocks away. She got there late in the afternoon, as a woman stood inside sweeping up chunks of fallen hair. Maria asked her if she could help her out. The woman, whose name was Laverne, asked her if she needed a weave.

Maria considered this option, then said no.

Laverne looked relieved and said okay, she could help her out, as long as it didn't involve a weave. She could do a perm. That was easy.

A whole lot of formaldehyde later, Maria looked different. The curls came out a little tighter than she'd hoped, more "On the Good Ship Lollipop" than "Oh What a Feeling." And Laverne insisted on giving her gold highlights at the tips.

Maria doesn't hate the highlights. She thinks they soften her features. She and Laverne agreed that the little bit of gold made her skin appear less sallow than it did before, a euphemism if Maria had ever heard one.

And the curls, Laverne assured her, would relax after she washed them.

It turned into a longer afternoon at the salon than she'd planned. As Laverne stood teasing her curls, Maria made the mistake of telling her that she was getting her hair done in preparation for a big first date.

Oh, Laverne said, smiling saucily as she sprayed something on Maria's curls. In that case, we better get you cleaned up. Mikki!

Maria had thought they were alone, but then a fat white woman emerged from behind a curtain. Laverne ordered Mikki to wax Maria's brows into high arches, get rid of her mustache and her leg hair and most of her genital hair.

Mikki, smirking, led Maria to the back room and ordered her to strip.

Mikki did this little thing where she smacked Maria's skin hard in one spot before she pulled the wax off another spot. She said it was a trick she'd learned in beauty school—

to create a distraction on one part of the body so the pain of the waxing would be lessened. It sort of worked, but Maria now had red slap marks all over her body.

She isn't displeased with what Laverne and Mikki did to her. Her body feels more human—less simian—beneath her clothes. And the curls make her look more biracial than she did before. They do soften her features. They do indeed make her look less sallow. She wishes Gloria could see her with the curls. She looks a crumb closer to her mother. They could actually be mother and daughter, biologically, with the curls. She could almost—if she was a little bit younger—be a girl in a music video with these curls. The girls in the videos always have these curls.

But in the light of the hallway, Khalil's expression is one of alarm.

What did you do to your hair?

She touches her hair. I got a perm.

Ethan, Khalil says, turning to his friend. Meet my poodle—I mean my fiancée.

He always talks like this around Ethan—sarcastic and corny jokes fly between them.

Maria shrugs. They'll relax after I wash them.

I should hope so, he says, patting her hair gingerly.

His lips are curled into a mocking smile for Ethan's sake, but his eyes, she can see, are shining and scared.

Are they going to last until the wedding? he asks.

Maria says, I haven't decided.

She hears a kind of Kitty Genovese scream out in the night. Waits for more but it is followed by silence.

Khalil stares at her for a moment, tight-lipped. Did you ever call back the woman at the Beach Plum Inn? She left another message.

I'm going to call her tomorrow.

Khalil walks with his head down to the bathroom and shuts the door hard behind him.

She looks at Ethan and says, Sheesh, what's gotten into him? Khalil never takes a second cup of coffee at home.

Ethan doesn't laugh at her joke. They stare at each other in thick silence before Maria heads to the kitchen to fix herself a drink.

Ethan follows her and stands at the doorway, his arms folded, watching her.

Did I see you a week ago pushing a baby stroller in the Village?

No.

I could have sworn I saw you there—

It wasn't me.

Maria takes a gulp of wine. It is old and tastes like vinegar. She spits it into the sink, and begins to search around the refrigerator for a new bottle. She finds one and sets to opening it at the counter, her eyes fixed on the bottle, not Ethan.

Maria, don't lie to me.

I'm not lying.

Ethan is a tall man with a wide strapping chest. He's grown a beard and it makes him appear like a lumberjack. His form seems to take up the whole kitchenette. He seems bigger and wider than she remembered him.

During their fight about Woody Allen so many years ago she had the feeling he was struggling not to punch her in the face. His face got very red as he belted out the names of Woody Allen movies, rapid-fire, asking her one after another if she really didn't think they were funny. *Annie Hall. Manhattan. Zelig.* He tilted his body toward her, his fists balled up at his sides. At some point, mid-fight, she remembered that she did in fact find Woody Allen movies funny—all of the ones she'd ever seen—but it was too late to back down and it wasn't the point. She wanted to have the right not to find them funny.

She told Khalil later that she'd felt physically threatened by Ethan.

Khalil said she was being paranoid. He said Ethan was a feminist and would never hit a woman.

When she insisted he was violent, Khalil said, He's the child of classics professors, for God's sake.

Now he is hovering beside her in the kitchenette, taking up a lot of room. He's making her uncomfortable.

Make yourself at home, she says to him, nodding toward the living room. Remote control's in there.

He doesn't move.

He speaks beside her in a low, tight voice: Here's the thing, Maria. I know I saw you with a stroller. I was standing across the street and it was dark, but I saw you. I called your name but you didn't hear me. You looked like you were in a real hurry. I am absolutely sure it was you. I asked Khalil about it and he didn't know what I was talking about.

It was just somebody who looked like me.

No, it was definitely you. You without this—Afro.

Maria jerks around to stare at him.

Here's the other thing, Maria. I love Khalil like a brother. Okay? So if you hurt him, you are going to have to contend with me.

You're joking, right? I mean this whole mafia don shtick.

Did you just say "shtick"?

She turns away and begins to wash a bowl from the ramen she ate earlier. There are noodles trapped in the drain. They look like bits of brain. She hears Khalil coming out of the bathroom, the toilet flushing behind him. Hears his bright jostling white-boy voice. What are you two kittens conspiring about?

Nothing, man. Just shooting the shit.

Turn on the game, get a brewski. Come on, dude. It's the playoffs.

She can hear the boy Khalil once was, a long time ago, before her. Before he began to drop his g's and pepper his sentences with that eternally rhetorical question: Know what I'm sayin'? She can hear the only black guy at the frat party—the Hootie in his Blowfish—that still lives inside of him.

Ethan leaves the kitchen and she can hear them joking around, settling into their seats side by side.

She is trembling. She really thinks Ethan is dangerous. Violent. Or at least potentially so. He only gets away with it because he's a big white man with a fancy pedigree. Later she will say these words to Khalil.

For now, she goes to the bedroom and shuts the door.

She takes some deep breaths. Tries to calm down. She has work to do. Tomorrow she will see the poet. The thought of it makes Ethan and the whole world feel very far away. She begins to rifle through her closet until she finds her favorite dress. It is shaped like a child's old-fashioned pinafore, black and woolen and hitting just above her knees. She will wear it when she meets the poet. She will pair it with bright pink stockings and low-heeled boots. She lays all the pieces out on the bed like a paper doll outfit, the waist of the tights hidden beneath the skirt of the dress and the legs stretching down beneath the boots. It almost looks like a real person lying there.

R*endezvous.* That's the word she keeps thinking of. *Rendezvous.* Today is the day of their rendezvous. She rides the subway all dressed up in her outfit, her vagina bald and her head hair curly. She sees herself in the subway glass and thinks how she looks like a different Maria.

She arrives at the bar ten minutes early. She had hoped to arrive ten minutes late, breathless and windswept, but her timing was off. The poet has not yet arrived. She takes a seat at the bar. The bartender asks her what she wants. She says, Scotch and milk. The bartender stares at her for a moment as if he thinks she's joking. She repeats the order. She has never ordered a Scotch and milk in her life but she has always wondered. The bartender places the cloudy liquid before her. She takes a gulp and it is sharp tasting, bitter. She'd hoped it would be milkier. It will not soothe the roiling in her stomach.

The bar is not crowded. It is only late afternoon and outside the rain is falling in steady gray sheets over the West Village. A few people sit on low couches near the window, looking out onto the street.

She checks her watch. The poet is officially seven minutes late. She thinks he is probably trying to stage a windswept entrance. He's actually going to pull it off.

She could have a good life if the poet never shows up. A Brooklyn brownstone, a tribe of butterscotch dream children, a fancy tenure-track job based on her book on the ethnomusicology of the Peoples Temple, so what if nobody except the faculty on her graduate committee ever reads it, summers spent in Martha's Vineyard, chatting with megastar intellectuals on private sand. She thinks about how she could enter the world that eluded Gloria.

Gloria. The French have an expression for when somebody suddenly ages. They call it "the blow of age." *Le coup de vieux*. Poverty, Maria knows, can show up on you quite suddenly too.

Around Gloria's eighth year in the PhD program, living off student loans, trying to feed Maria and finish her dissertation and teach adjunct courses, she woke up one day and looked poor. It wasn't about money. It was a particular kind of bag-lady aura that infects PhD students who are overdue on student loans. Her Afro had gone untended for too long. It was past the point of looking political. Her tortoiseshell glasses, once stylish, were taped together at one temple, and the lenses were scratched and filmy. She had begun to wear the same uniform every day, a uniform for working on a computer and schlepping back and forth to the library, sweatpants and an oversized cardigan that had pilled up into a million balls of acrylic fiber. A uniform for going to work on something you know, in your heart of hearts, is not moving forward. Her left front tooth was beginning to rot and she didn't have the dental insurance plan to deal with it.

Maria looked poor too. She was only seven at the time, but in photos she had the look of one of the Roma you see on the streets of Paris. Her hair was always tangled, her pants too short, a perpetual stain of dirt and lollipop juice around the rim of her mouth. Harvard notwithstanding, she lived like any other poor child on a steady diet of hot dogs and ramen noodles. She lived in a cement tower that looked—if you blurred your eyes just right—like any other housing project.

One day, Gloria was standing with Maria outside Café Algiers in Harvard Square. She was holding her coffee cup with no lid—trying to let the scalding liquid cool off before she took the first sip—when a couple approached them. They were a white man and a white woman and they were deep in conversation. The woman was blond, wearing a long wool coat. Maria noticed the woman looking at Gloria as they approached. She didn't seem to notice Maria, so fixed was her gaze on Gloria. As she and the man walked past, the woman held out her hand and dumped a handful of change into Gloria's coffee. The scalding liquid splashed out, burning Gloria's hand. The couple kept walking, not even noticing the mistake.

Gloria stared into the cup, where the change the woman had thrown in had sunk to the bottom.

Did that actually just happen? she finally managed to say.

Maria nodded. Motherfuckers.

Gloria glanced at Maria, about to chastise her for her language, then thought better of it. She threw her cup down and started to walk in a swift rage after the couple. Maria followed at Gloria's heels. She was half excited, half dreading the fight that was about to occur. Gloria got right up behind them, almost upon them, but then stopped, stepped back, a startled look on her face.

They're getting away, Maria said, pointing at the couple, who were moving into the throngs of revelers in the Friday night Square. You're gonna lose them.

Gloria looked tired. I'm never going to finish this book, am I? I'm never going to get out of this program alive.

Her mother looked so frail standing there. Maria could

see the lanky young woman she'd once been, the one she'd only seen in photographs, her eyes twinkling with irony, her mouth twisted into a smirk.

Gloria used to drag Maria everywhere. From the special collections stacks to conference halls, from seminar tables to department mixers, Maria went with her mother to everything. Gloria would set her up with a book and a pad of paper in the corner of some non-child-friendly space. She used to try to make it a game for Maria. She'd whisper to her, They all think you're a child prodigy. Nobody knows you're my daughter. Maria got into the act. She would affect what she imagined was the expression of a child genius, precocious and slightly tragic, as she trailed after her mother, trying to catch the eyes of passing students, to imagine herself through their eyes.

It is clear to Maria now, sipping the Scotch and milk at the bar, why Gloria never finished her dissertation. Because she had a child. She had Maria. The child was a weight on her mother's ankle. No words on a page can compete for attention with a demanding child. She once overheard Gloria saying to her best friend at the kitchen table, See, when you adopt a baby you're their first wound. Don't buy this bullshit about it being a blessing. You're not their mother. You don't smell like home. You don't smell like the body. So you have to lay it on thick. Be right up beside them until they forget that other body. Until they are so smothered by your love they don't even fucking remember her.

Maria feels a gray figure hovering beside her. It's here. It's in the bar. She feels its warmth and weight. But when she looks up at the door she sees it is not the gray thing that has entered the room. It is him. The poet. He walks inside the bar and stands looking around for her. He has no hair so he isn't exactly windswept, but the effect is the same.

She waits for him to see her, her whole body pulsing. She thinks about the time she saw Elizabeth Taylor in the flesh at a Barneys perfume counter. This is so much more than that. Like she is witnessing something from a dream or a movie become reality. Something impossible becoming possible. He is wearing an army-green parka. His head is hatless. He glimpses her and seems not to recognize her for a moment. He looks away, scans the room, then back at her, frowing. She lifts a hand.

He nods, starts across the room in her direction.

You look different, he says, eyeing her with mild suspicion.

She touches her hair. I'm not—different.

Did you always have curls?

She looks away. I usually wear it straight.

She wonders if by her answer—I usually wear it straight—he will think she usually straightens her hair and that these curls are her hair's natural state. She is pleased at the thought of this confusion, and glancing at her reflection behind the bar, almost believes it—that this curly-haired girl is her "going natural."

He sits down. So, do you have my hat?

She hesitates, waiting for him to laugh. It's got to be a joke that he is already asking for the hat. But he just watches her, unsmiling. Her eyes stinging, she opens her purse and pulls out the hat. She stares at it for a brief moment before handing it over to him, feeling a sinking unhappiness as the transfer is made.

Thanks, he says, shoving it into his jacket pocket. She is afraid he's going to get up and go now, but when the bartender comes over and asks him what he wants, he asks the bartender what kind of beer they serve. She feels all her muscles relax. He is staying. He was just getting their business out of the way. It was a pretense, enacted for both their sakes.

She listens as he and the bartender proceed to have a very lengthy conversation. He asks the bartender specific questions about each kind of beer on the menu, and the bartender answers him with utmost seriousness, as if he has been waiting his whole life to have this conversation with somebody. Finally the poet decides on a pale ale from Belgium and the bartender assures him he's made a great choice.

They drink. They don't talk about personal matters. They talk about movies and books, people and places, their preferences and hatreds. She longs to ask him more personal questions, but doesn't. And anyway, from this conversation she gleans everything she needs to know. They are meant for each other. They have strange, unlikely things in common. They both like the music of Steely Dan and Roberta Flack and DJ Quik and Del the Funky Homosapien. They both think that song by Shuggie Otis, "Strawberry Letter 23," contains the best first few minutes to any song, ever. They both enjoy reading books by Evelyn Waugh and Chester Himes and graphic novels by Kyle Baker and they both love the movies of Roman Polanski. They both listen to Joni Mitchell, and secretly, they both sometimes listen to James Taylor, though not without a certain feeling of humiliation. And she wants the poet to know that since he mentioned it to her that day in front of the record shop, she has decided that she too dislikes Brooklyn. She tells him she thinks it has "bad vibes"—and that maybe underneath, it's a Native American sacred burial ground.

Like, it's somewhere we shouldn't be living at all, she says.

He nods, agrees. He has had this exact thought too.

Strangest, most telling of all, they both harbor the same exact fantasy about moving out of the city to the Hudson River Valley, settling down in the same exact town called Snedens Landing, where neither of them has ever been but have seen on maps.

Maria's face hurts from smiling. She thinks of a line from a Dr. Seuss book she used to love as a child. *We are here, we are here, we are here.*

The poet nods toward a sofa in front of the fireplace and asks if she wants to sit over there. Yes, she says, adding, like they do in movies: Let's get more comfortable. They carry their things across the bar, which has grown more crowded. She realizes, walking behind him, that she is a little drunk and happier than she has been in many months, maybe years. They sit side by side on the velvet sofa. He holds a fresh pint of the Belgian pale ale in his hand.

They have not discussed or even mentioned Khalil the whole time they've been talking. But once they are seated by the fire, something changes. The poet looks at her and says: So, are you and Khalil going to have those little figurines on top of your wedding cake? Do they even make them with dreadlocks?

She stares into her glass. I don't know, she says in a quiet, serious voice. She understands what he is doing. He is trying to make light of a painful situation. She turns to look out at the gray evening light. There are ancient dirty snow piles in the tree beds outside. In the distance, a tiny dog is taking a shit. The world beyond the window looks like a hard, cold place. She wants to stay inside this bar forever, the fire warming her skin, the poet beside her. But she thinks with a kind of weary resolve how many steps she has to take—how much unraveling she needs to do before she can get to the other side.

She feels his hand touch her shoulder. He gives her a gentle push.

Hey, he says. Come on. Tell me about the wedding. Are you gonna wear one of those froufrou white dresses? Write your own vows? Are you gonna hold your glass of champagne and interlink arms with him and do that thing where they take a sip all tangled up like that?

He is wearing a teasing, big brotherly smile, and she thinks he is making fun of her.

Come on, he says. Spill the beans. Are you gonna go on a honeymoon to Paree?

Don't do this, she says. Please.

Do what? He takes a gulp of beer. Hey, have I mentioned how much I hate Paris? I went last year. Nothing new is ever going to happen in that city. It's over.

I hate it too, she says. Though she has never been, she imagines she will hate it too.

The music playing from the loudspeakers is a Hall and Oates song she hasn't heard in a long time. "Sara Smile." Maria says, I love this song. Don't you?

He shrugs. I don't know about love. It's not bad. It's true they don't make white boys like that anymore.

Are they white? I thought one of them was black.

He makes air quotes with his fingers and says, Sicilian.

His hand lies on the sofa only inches from her own. His knuckles are knobby and his fingers ringless. She has already decided that if he invites her back to his apartment she will go. The chances of her bumping into Susan are slim, and even if she does, she suspects Susan won't recognize her with her curly hair. And even if she does recognize her, Maria will deny everything. Nobody will believe Susan's story, because it doesn't make sense.

She starts to inch her hand slowly across the velvet toward his, but he lifts his hand abruptly and checks his watch.

Shit, he says. It's getting late.

She tries to sound casual. Should we find something to eat? She says it but she knows she won't be able to eat. She doesn't want to be with him for the first time on a full stomach.

I can't tonight, he says. He looks at his watch again and chugs downs the rest of his beer.

She swallows. A hard ball has formed in her throat. Wait, she croaks. You have plans?

He is wearing a distant smile. You could say that. I'm meeting someone for dinner.

She scratches her arm. A girl?

Yeah, a girl, he says, looking down at the floor, bashful now. It's all really early. We'll see. He sighs. We're just hanging out. I'm not all grown up like you, with your wedding planner and your big fancy ring.

She realizes, with a mounting bitter clarity, that he is confiding in her. He thinks she is his confidant—the equivalent of the fat girl sidekick or the gay best friend in a movie.

The fire is crackling, the flames gone suddenly high. Her eyes sting as she stares into its burning glow. She rubs at her eyes with her fists. She hears his voice, as if from a great distance, asking if she's okay. She says there is an ash in her eye and excuses herself. Inside the restroom she pees. Her genitals look so strange and ridiculous with no hair. When she pulls up her tights she sees that they have a giant run in the back leading up and under her skirt. She paces the ladies' room trying to control her breathing. She doesn't know where to go. She is drunk but not drunk enough. She needs more Scotch and milk. She looks at herself in the mirror. Her curls are no longer tight neat coils. A top layer of frizz has formed around her head like a haze of gnats. Laverne never told her it would do that. Maria makes herself grin at her reflection, then frowns. She says aloud, I hate you.

■ ■ ■

The poet is standing by the exit when she comes out. He's wearing his parka and the Pittsburgh Steelers cap.

So he did want the hat back, she thinks. It wasn't just trash after all.

He is holding her coat and purse like a gentleman. I already settled up, he says. You can get me next time.

Out on the street, it is warmer than she expected. There is a sound of running water and she realizes the snow piles are melting.

Man, he says, it's gonna be spring before we know it. He nudges her and says in a wispy girl voice, Wedding season.

She hails a cab. One immediately screeches to a stop for her and the poet says, drolly, Look at that—the privilege of membership.

He smiles at her when he says it, as if they will laugh together, but she can't muster even a smile. Her throat feels raw as if she has been in a primal scream workshop. The poet leans in to hug her goodnight. He smells of laundry detergent.

When he steps away, he says, You look like somebody— I can't think who it is.

She fixes her face into what she hopes is a blank expression. She can't remember how to speak.

He reaches forward and ruffles her curls. Laughs a little as if he thinks her hair is somehow funny. You okay?

She manages a twist of her lips she hopes looks like a smile. She makes a gorilla-like sound. Uh. Uh.

He gives her one last perplexed look, then waves and walks away with the hat on his head toward his true destination. She watches his retreating form, the stark shame of what has occurred washing over her. He has been only half present with her all evening. While she sat in a kind of heady bliss, mooning over their every similarity, he was only half there, his mind on this other person he has gone off to share a meal with, or worse. It was a hat drop-off. Nothing more. She wonders if the other girl shares his feelings about Steely Dan and Evelyn Waugh and Snedens Landing. It seems impossible. And yet he is heading off to her, this other girl with whom he shares nothing. He has missed everything. She has failed to make him see.

The cab beside her beeps. The driver is waiting. She slips inside and slams the door.

Brooklyn, she says.

The driver groans. You gotta be fucking kidding me.

I'm not fucking kidding, she says, and slumps down low in the seat. She can smell her own funk wafting up from inside her jacket. The cab lurches forward. Voices speak from the radio in a language she does not understand.

■　■　■

Khalil is asleep in the bedroom. It is still dark outside. She sits curled in a blanket in the living room. The voices on the radio beside her are talking about a rapper who died tonight. Four bullet wounds to his neck and chest. They are playing his music on continuous loop. Maria listens for a while before she shuts it off.

Her whole body aches. It is still so early. She should go back to bed, but she knows she will not be able to sleep.

Instead she puts on the video of the last night at Jonestown and sits watching it in the gray dusk light. She has seen it so many times before. The footage is grainy. The people in it stand around the pavilion. They are waiting for Congressman Ryan, who is visiting tonight. They are waiting to show him they are happy there. They want to show him their experiment was a success. They want him to know they did it—they created Another America. The place they'd advertised in the pamphlet years before had become a reality.

She watches the footage from the sofa. A woman stands onstage singing a strained warbling version of Earth, Wind and Fire's "That's the Way of the World" while the crowd dances and claps. The singer has a beautiful voice.

Her name is Deanna Wilkinson. Maria knows her story. Knows she was born in 1950, the daughter of a white woman and a black man. When she was very small her parents fought and one of them threw a pan of burning oil at the other, but it splashed the girl instead. Deanna's face was badly burned. She was removed from her parents' custody. Deanna was one of the Eternally Wounded. She'd been born even before Elsa. Even before the Era of Mulatto Martyrs. She had been born in the Dark Ages of Mestizo Abandonment. While one side of her face was scarred from the burn, the other side remained smooth and untouched. She roamed from one temporary shelter to another until she found Jim Jones. He saved her life. He told her to get on the Greyhound bus and go with him to California. She followed him there and she followed him to Guyana. She never gave up on Jim Jones and she never stopped being ashamed of the scars on one side of her face.

On that final night at Jonestown, while the old people

smiled their stiff smiles and danced their stiff dances, Deanna sang Earth, Wind and Fire.

In the video, Congressman Ryan at one point gets onstage. He looks exactly like an actor Maria has seen in made-for-television movies. His wording is careful, awkward. He says into the microphone that the few people he has spoken to that evening have expressed to him that this place is the best thing that had ever happened to them. Before he can say more, the crowd drowns him out with wild, unending applause. He tries to continue with his speech, but the crowd is manic—the applause has the sound of a kind of silencing mob drown-out more than approval.

There is a tarnished, macabre quality to the footage. If you look past the smiles, the dancing, the laughter, the people in the crowd look tired and dirty and thin and coated in a layer of jungle sweat. They are malnourished. Their joy and applause feel manic and desperate. Jim Jones has been coaching them for weeks, teaching them how to make a work camp look like a socialist utopia. He has fed them well for the first time in a year. He has told them to pick something nice to wear from the pile of communal clothing. They have done a good job of pretending, but it is there, if you look closely. It is there in certain shots, when Maria freezes the footage.

Outside, the light in the sky is brightening, edging toward morning. Jim Jones is speaking on camera, his eyes hidden behind his signature sunglasses. He is speaking directly to the cameraman, the one he will murder at the air-strip later.

People play games, friend, he is saying. They lie. They lie. What can I do about liars? Anybody wants to get out of here can get out of here. They have no problem about getting out of here. They come and go all the time.

■ ■ ■

Maria does not see the poet again. She does not try to see him. She has moved forward and thrown herself full-body into the future she has chosen with Khalil. She finally returns that call to the woman at the Beach Plum Inn. She discusses the floral arrangements with a woman in Boston. She hires a deejay for the after-party they are throwing at the converted hangar at the Martha's Vineyard airport. She peruses the caterer's menu of nouveau soul food and checks off her selections for the rehearsal dinner.

And though that day at Bergdorf's she did not settle on

a wedding dress, she finds the perfect dress by accident one afternoon. She's on her way to the public library, where she is going to make copies of the FBI transcripts from Jonestown. She is on 31st Street, in the Garment District, when she glances up and does a double take. Inside the window, a dark-haired mannequin stands somewhat jauntily, with her hands on her hips, beneath an awning that reads Jaymi Bride. Maria stands outside just looking at her for a while before going inside.

All the salesladies are Korean and don't speak much English. One steps forward and introduces herself as Emily. She asks what she can do for Maria.

Maria points to the mannequin in the window. I try that? She catches herself. It is one of Khalil's pet peeves about her—the way she always speaks in broken English when addressing people with strong accents. She speaks to them as if she too can't form proper sentences. She corrects herself now. I'd like to try on that dress, she says to Emily. That one right there.

Muzak plays over the speakers. Emily is dressed in a pencil skirt and panty hose, low heels, like a shopgirl from the 1950s. What was it Gloria used to say? Nobody does Americana like new immigrants.

Emily helps her get the dress. She and another saleswoman have to drag the mannequin onto her side to get her out of the window. Maria stands off to the side, a little tense as she watches them unscrewing the arms and hoisting the dress off of the figure.

It is not the dress Maria expected to want. The dresses she saw at Bergdorf's were more what she would have imagined herself wearing. Those were classy numbers. This dress is something else. It is full-skirted, ivory, with a jewel-encrusted V-necked bodice. It is dreamy—a confection made in Seoul. The shopgirls help her get it on in the softly lit dressing room area.

Afterward, Maria turns in slow circles in front of the mirror, admiring herself, wondering what Gloria would think if she could see her now.

She brings Lisa back to the store a few days later to see the dress. Maria makes sure to invite Oma on today's outing, since she's paying for the dress, but Oma says over the phone that she is too old and tired to drag her aching bones across town again. She says, Pick the dress that makes you happy, Maria. Just have them call me when it's time to pay.

Maria meets Lisa outside the subway station at 34th and Broadway. They have made up since their nefarious meeting in the ladies' room. Lisa has received her real present, the Lisa Doll by Ceres, and loved it as much as Khalil had imagined she would. The doll really does look like Lisa. It even wears a miniature indigo head wrap. She keeps it propped in her dining room, its arm around a bottle of gin. Nobody has ever mentioned Stacy Lattisaw again.

Lisa comes out of the station looking tired, in faded jeans, an army jacket, a red kerchief on her head. She says she's just finished an eight-hour shift at the bakery. She says she's ready for art school. I'm done with the pastry chef shit, she says, wearily. Now let me see what you've got.

When they arrive at the shop, Lisa says, Seriously?

Maria ignores the question and leads her inside, where Emily is waiting, her hair in a flawless flip. She has been expecting Maria. She helps Maria change into the dress again. Lisa, slumped in a velour armchair, doesn't say anything when Maria steps out from behind the curtain. She just stares at her, a tight smile on her face.

Emily stands behind Lisa and holds up a finger, swirls it in circles to suggest that Maria should also turn in circles. So she does, her arms sticking straight out by her sides. Afterward Emily squats on her hands and knees beside Maria, her brow furrowed, sticking pins into the gown's hem.

Too over-the-top? Maria says to Lisa, who has still not spoken.

Well. Lisa crosses her arms. Well. Um. Wow.

Well, um, wow, what?

Okay. You do realize nobody wears that style anymore, right? She glances around the store, laughs a little. I mean, it's all about clean lines—the simple satin sheath. Not—that.

Oh. Maria swallows, embarrassed now.

But, Lisa says. She rises from the chair and goes to stand before Maria. You know what else?

What?

I fucking love it, she says. I think it's genius.

Really?

Really. I love how over-the-top, princess fantasy it is. Like you're channeling your inner six-year-old girl. It's— it's so bad it's good.

Maria turns to look at her reflection. She hadn't meant it as an ironic gesture.

Lisa nods. I think we should do it. Let's do it.

Afterward, they go out to dinner together at a nearby restaurant. Over bowls of steaming bibimbap, Lisa describes the cake she is designing for the bakery in Martha's Vineyard. It's going to be over-the-top like Maria's dress, she says—four-tiered, mint hand-piped royal icing, details of shimmery gold luster dust.

■ ■ ■

Maria is relieved to have the dress search over. There are six weeks till the wedding—and less than four weeks till her dissertation is due. Though she knows dissertation deadlines are meant to be missed (oh boy, does she know) she wants it to be over before the wedding. She wants to float down the aisle in her Korean confection, free from

Jonestown. She doesn't feel so much done with Jonestown
as she feels ready to be done with Jonestown. It isn't that
she has said all that she needs to say about the music of the
Peoples Temple. It is, rather, that she is finally accepting
that there will never be enough to say about it.

She is beginning to understand that completion is not so
much about reaching perfection as it is making the choice
to look away from the material. What was it Khalil used to
say when she couldn't finish a paper in college? Be a com-
pletionist, not a perfectionist. Gloria was a perfectionist. It
wasn't that she didn't have the stamina to finish her dissertation on Zora Neale Hurston and the triple consciousness
of black women protagonists; it was that she could not
tear herself away from the material. She couldn't bear to
leave Janie behind. Because Gloria understood that to finish something—to make something right and final—is to
kill it.

The longer Maria looks at the people of Jonestown, listens to their voices, and stares at the pictures of their smiling hopeful faces, the more she can see that there is no way
to say enough about them. Maria can see now that it is ar-
bitrary, in a way—when you decide to stop looking at a
thing, to put down your pen and walk away. The meanings
will continue to form inside you, but you can make the
choice to turn your gaze elsewhere.

Her mentor was encouraging in their last correspon-
dence. He wrote to her from Berkeley, where he'd gone for

his sabbatical. He said he'd read her most recent pages and that he thought she was making progress—he believed that her work was almost done.

Maria is clearer about a lot of things these days. She knows now that the poet—everything that has gone on between them—happened entirely in her own head. She has the sense of having gotten away with something—of some danger narrowly averted. And she wonders if she is getting religious because these days, whenever she sees the crazy Creole woman who wanders their block, dressed all in white, raving, she thinks of the phrase "There but for the grace of God go I."

Still. She must be careful. Abstinence is the best policy. Lisa calls one evening and invites her and Khalil to a night of poetry and music with her in the city. Khalil, holding the phone to his ear, asks Maria if she wants to go. It's at the Fez. She hesitates. Khalil says, with a shrug, that the poet will be reading.

He says it as if it is just a simple detail about somebody they vaguely know, as if this detail will help her make her mind up—because he likes the poet, he enjoys his poetry. He says it as if this might be a fun thing for them to do together. Watch the poet read his poems.

There but for the grace of God go I.

Maria says that she feels like staying home tonight. Would that be okay? If we just stay home?

Khalil says, That's fine, babe, and tells Lisa that they

are staying home. He hangs up and throws some nuts in his mouth and says, Lisa says we're already acting like an old married couple. Then he sits down and turns up the volume on the TV. It's *Seinfeld*. George Costanza is screaming. His face has turned blue. She's seen this one before. And for a moment, watching it, seated beside Khalil, she is in the danger zone again. She feels a tightness in her breath. She rises and walks down the hall and locks herself inside the bathroom and strips off her clothes and climbs into the empty bathtub naked. She sits inside the empty porcelain bowl hugging her knees and rocking back and forth.

The other girl will likely be at the reading tonight—the girl he went off to meet, despite the obvious and uncanny connection between him and Maria. He will read aloud his poems and the other girl will sit under the dim light of the Fez wearing a private smile.

Maria is shivering now.

Khalil knocks.

Should we scare up some dinner, babe?

Yes. Yes. I'm coming right out.

They cook. They actually cook. Not like an old married couple but like a newly married couple that will never become dreary or old. They make risotto with white wine and asparagus. It is delicious. They eat it in front of *My Beautiful Laundrette* and afterward they have sex on the living room shag rug. It is the first time they've done it on this rug. She reminds herself as he hovers over her that it's not so bad. It's just a penis inside a vagina, an ancient and whole-some pairing, like cookies and milk. It makes babies. It isn't that deep. She will make it to the other side.

Khalil falls asleep beside her on the rug, and she lies in the semidarkness, thinking that the poet is probably mak-ing love to the other girl in his little apartment right now. The other girl who is probably a fan of his poetry, who probably has memorized his poems. Maria feels numb at the thought of this, actually numb, which seems, surely, like a kind of progress.

Besides. She loves Khalil. She likes him and loves him. He's the man on her wedding cake. He's the Jimmy and the Johnny of her girlhood daydreams. They make a fine pic-ture together walking down the street, holding hands.

Once upon a time, Greg, not yet Goya, asked her, wist-fully, while tracing a finger along her body, What if the world got so mixed up there was no black and white? Ever think of that?

Don't be an idiot, she'd said to him. It's called Brazil. And you want to know something about Brazil? Those motherfuckers coined the phrase "Money whitens." So don't talk to me about race mixing. 'Cause it won't solve shit.

Greg, not yet Goya, also said to her once, I've always thought mixed people were the prettiest. I've always thought it was, like, God's way of telling us we should mix.

She just stared at him that time, fighting the urge to hit

him over the head with a small African statuette she kept beside her bed.

But maybe he was onto something in his imbecilic we-are-the-world revelations. She's tired of being smart. Maybe she and Khalil are some kind of solution—the beautiful blend that happens four hundred years after humanity's collision. What's black and white and red all over? America. The bloody triumvirate. She and Khalil are what happens when colors mix and then mix again and then again.

Okay, so the sex is not great, but in Maria's mind she's already skipped to the part where they don't have sex anymore. She's done the math. Apparently they don't have that many years of good sex left. Once they have kids, it's all downhill—sex that is at best pathetic, at worst, a chore. And Khalil says he wants to try to get pregnant as soon as they are married. So the years of bad sex that are specific to them are not much longer. Soon it will be generalized, married-with-children bad sex. And everyone else they hang around with will also have kids and also be having bad sex, or no sex at all, so she will end up in the same place as the rest of them, no matter who she marries.

Maria feels grateful to Khalil for showing up when he did. She is acutely aware that there were always other options—other story lines she could have chosen or inherited or stumbled into. Khalil has spared her from all of these other stories. In his arms she is, as Gloria would say, a radical departure from the obvious scripts for a mixed girl born the year she was born.

Scenario One. She ends up with a white boy. Not Greg. An ordinary white boy. A perfectly good white boy. The kind you don't throw out with the trash. Let's call this white boy Dave. Let's say Maria marries Dave. She never feels as black as she does in Dave's arms. When she clears his dishes, she says she feels like his slave. So Dave clears the dishes. She says she feels like his slave when she mops the floor. So Dave mops the floor. She imagines he is raping her when he makes love to her. Dave is anything but a rapist—but still, it's there, in the back of her mind when they have sex, that he is a rapist. And she tells him and he hears her and after that he's very tender during lovemaking and asks her for permission before he does each and every thing.

With Dave, Maria runs the show. She is the beloved, he is the lover. Every couple has one of each. If she and Dave ever broke up, she knows and he knows he will never go back to the other side. He will only ever again be with women as dark or darker than Maria. It's true what they say: Once you go black, you never go back, even if your black was kind of white. Maria is his island in the sun. She is his Dorothy Dandridge. She is his Gauguin girl in the tropical skirt. She loves and despises Dave in equal measure. It is a happy marriage.

She and Dave accrue the trappings of a middle-class life.

Turns out everyone who is somebody loves an interracial couple. She benefits from their association. She learns how to be around white people in a way that works for everyone. She learns to wear the smile, the one she's seen all her life on the faces of those brown women married to white men. A smile that is tight and lost and a little bewildered. A smile that wonders, Did I win the lottery or lose it? She convinces herself it does not bother her, coming home from a dinner party on the arm of this particular body, walking past the brown boys clustered on the street corner, feeling Dave's fear as they move past all the dark male bodies she has failed to embrace.

Let's say this is Maria's story. She develops a laugh that is light and more impulsive-sounding than it needs to be, the kind of laughter that puts white people at ease in her presence. She is the one they are referring to when they say "some of my best friends are black." She is the exception to the rule. She is the one they feel safe around. She adds flora and fauna to their dinner parties, but sometimes, still, they "forget" she is black. She has to remind them in small, non-threatening ways.

She gives birth to children lighter than herself (who knew that was possible!), children who someday grow up to go to the best colleges. On their applications, they put down that they are "everything." Because it's true. There is no one-drop rule anymore. And only now that that rule is gone does Maria realize how much she has depended on it for her survival. And only now that her children are grown does she realize that what the lady says in the Tide commercial is true: You actually can wash out a stain. It wasn't as stubborn as you were led to believe. You really can get those clothes white again. And once the stain is gone it is really gone.

And she thinks perhaps it doesn't bother her. She is everything she set out to be. She is loved. She is happy.

And then one day she notices a pain in her throat when she swallows. She feels a lump there, on her neck, a firm bulge under her skin. Now what is this? And she wonders if the lump there has to do with all the times she swallowed her words. If it has to do with her practiced easy laugh. If it has to do with all the times she smiled so hard her face hurt.

No, the doctor assures her. This is just the way the cells divide. This is deeper than skin.

Dave makes love to her in the dark that night after her diagnosis. She thinks how in the blue light, hovering above her, he looks almost like a black man—the outline of a man who could be her father.

Scenario Two. The one where Maria stays true to her race. Oh, it's not pretty either. It ends the same way. She gets cornrows in her hair, but they won't stay neat. The braids keep coming loose. Her girlfriends think she's the funniest thing on earth. Dance for me, Maria, dance for me. She does the Smurf for them and they all bust up laughing. She speaks in exaggerated Ebonics. She jerks her neck and snaps her fingers and goes on Stokely Carmichael rants when the occasion calls. Later, after college, she has a string of buppie boyfriends—stiff weirdos in suits. They smell too much like cologne. (All of them tell her, at some point after the first date, that they have a crush on Vanessa Williams. She attracts that type of man. She realizes she looks nothing like Vanessa Williams. She realizes everything is a euphemism.)

The babies come one after another from three different guys, they come like dark waves from her pale body, each one there to make her feel she's crossed over for good.

Years later, after all the buppies have left her for white women, she turns into a churchgoing middle-aged spinster. She thinks she will find home in Jesus. Maybe He is the man she was looking for all these years. She sits in church weeping, surrounded by brown women and men who think of her as their little mascot. She is adored, she who has never talked back, never strayed. She is Gloria's daughter. She has become the daughter Gloria wanted, finally.

Then one day, there it is, the pain in her throat when she swallows. She wonders, has to wonder, if it has to do with all the times she pretended to hate white people. All the times she pretended to hate half of herself. If this lump has anything to do with all the times she has painted herself, her history, as blacker than somebody else's, in an attempt to gain membership. Pick me! Pick me! I'm the soldier you want. Could it have to do with that?

No, the doctor tells her, as they stand together staring at the X-rays on the glass—the shapes of problems growing beneath her skin. This abnormality he is seeing has nothing to do with any of that, the doctor says. It was always going to happen. No matter what.

What she and Khalil have been trying to pull off here— the audacity of it—is not lost on her.

■ ■ ■

Maria and Khalil wander Crate and Barrel one afternoon in a dream state, making a list of the objects they hope will fill their cabinets someday—fairly useless household items that, according to the saleslady at Crate and Barrel, are necessities of a grown-up, middle-class couple. Objects that nobody, as far as Maria can tell, uses on a daily basis, but they might someday whimsically desire, and should therefore have stored away in their cabinets just in case. A Le Creuset pie pan, fluted around the edges—because someday, once or twice in the next decade, she will want to bake a pie. A six-speed blender that can crush ice and probably fingers too in its silver blades. A Crock-Pot with a ceramic insert that promises to make wholesome dinners while the multitasking career mother is at work. A mortar and pestle made from volcanic rock used to crush spices for the slow-cooker meals she will someday prepare and leave to cook by themselves. A juicer for the fresh orange juice she will once or twice think to serve her tribe of racially nebulous children in the morning before school. A set of cocktail tumblers and a copper ice bucket for the chic parties they will do every weekend or more likely every few years. An ice cream machine, so they can, on a whim, make exotically flavored ice cream one Friday night after baking their own pizza using the portable Pizzeria Pronto oven. And a non-stick muffin tin too, because although she will not be the kind of dreary mother to slave over a hot stove every day, she will be the kind of woman who might decide to bake muffins once in a while just for fun. So she will have a muffin tin available when and if this should ever happen.

They celebrate the completion of their registry checklist by going out to lunch. Over matching Waldorf salads, Khalil says he has a surprise. He says, smiling, that he's contacted a friend at the *New York Times* who feels confident he can finagle a featured wedding announcement about them. Khalil says this means they will be the subject of a longer article, rather than just the blurbs with the headshots they give to everyone else.

We're going to be a fucking feature, he says.

Maria asks him why. He looks disappointed in her reaction.

I mean, she says, are we interesting enough for a feature? We met in college just like ninety-eight percent of the other couples in that section. What's so great about us?

Khalil leans across the table and whispers to her, We're mulatto. Everybody loves mulattos. Nobody will grow bored of us, ever.

He begins to laugh. She laughs too because it's funny. Every sentence is funnier with the word *mulatto* in it.

After lunch, they look into store windows, holding hands. She glimpses an attractive smiling couple up ahead. It's them, of course, a reflection in the glass. Maria and Khalil. They look good together. They really do. And she is happy with him. She thinks he's probably right about the article. They will be promoted to a feature story. They are already the subject of a documentary, after all. So what if the sex is not great. Nobody has to see their wooden love-making. That doesn't have to be in the feature article about them.

They only have to know this vision of them walking down a street laughing together. From far away they look like a couple that would have great sex. It's not that important—sex. The best sex she ever had was with a white guy she despised and fantasized about bludgeoning to death with an African statuette.

Elsa is going to shoot more footage for the film today. She has narrowed the film's focus to four New People. Maria and Khalil will be two of the four. The others will be a homeless rights activist in Berkeley who is half white and half black and also, predictably (and mathematically impossibly), part Cherokee. The other is an aspiring singer/actress who lives in Los Angeles and who is Nigerian and Swedish. All of them are around the same age, born in the late sixties and early seventies, the progeny of the Renaissance of Interracial Unions. Elsa says the film will intersperse interviews and footage of all four subjects—moving through their lives. She wants Maria and Khalil's story to be the narrative arc that holds the whole film together. She will reveal fairly early on that they are a couple but withhold that they are getting married until the very end.

It will, Elsa says, suggest the ending of an era, the beginning of a new one—like the way sometimes those apocalypse movies end with the birth of a baby. That will be implicit, that a new race will be born from these New People.

Maria and Khalil both know it is a big honor to be in the film, and especially to be the bookends for the story. Elsa has told them, in a conspiratorial whisper, that she chose them out of fifty other New People whom she auditioned.

Lisa isn't officially a subject in the film, but she shows up a lot on set, bringing pastries for the crew and standing with Ansel and Heidi, pointing out possible backdrops, rushing in to adjust Maria's scarf or arrange Khalil's dreadlocks. Elsa has promised her a cameo. Over Ethiopian food with them one night, she says, You do realize every mutt in the world is going to hate you guys when they see the movie. They're going to be, like, Who died and made these guys the Ministers of the Mulatto Nation?

Khalil laughs and assures Maria this isn't true. Nobody will hate them. Everyone will love them. And he points out the other benefit of being in the movie: They will be getting a professional-level camera crew to film their wedding, rather than having to pay out of pocket for a half-assed videographer. He's heard through the grapevine that Ansel is highly regarded as a documentary cameraman. Khalil says someday they can share the footage and the movie itself with their sons and their daughters, little Cheo and little Indigo. It will be a record of their life that they will someday cherish.

Maria has come around to seeing his point. But the film is eating up a lot of time. Elsa seems to need an astronomical amount of footage, filler shots of them together. Every weekend she wants to film something. Maria would prefer to be in the library in those moments, because she feels like a horse who smells the stable. Now that she knows she can finish, she wants to gallop toward that ending, rather than cavorting with Khalil in front of Elsa and Ansel in a variety of staged scenes. The long weekends away from her carrel feel disruptive at this late stage in the writing, and it always takes her a couple of days at the start of each week to immerse herself again. The momentum gets lost. But it seems important to Khalil that they fulfill their promise to Elsa. And he is actually enjoying their excursions on camera. So Maria puts her work aside every weekend to do it.

Today Elsa has planned for them to attend a circus that has come to town. Maria and Khalil weren't planning to go, but it's right in the neighborhood, so they agree. It is a relatively new all-black circus called the UniverSoul Circus. Maria has seen the posters around town for weeks. She stands in her room getting dressed for it, listening to Elsa

and Khalil and Ansel and the new gaffer, Heather, a white
woman who seems to have replaced Heidi, with slightly different features but an identical buzz cut.

They are all in the other room, talking while they wait
for her.

Heather is talking about how much she's learned working for Elsa and Ansel. Maria can hear her saying that she
never felt that she belonged to an actual race before college,
that she thought of herself as "just human," but now she understands that whiteness is a race. She is white. She understands that this whiteness affords her privilege she didn't
earn. She is calling it her "invisible backpack," the privilege
she carries around on her back every single day.

Maria only half listens to their voices as she opens up
a box from the back of her closet. Inside are a bunch of old
clothes—things she had planned to give to charity months
ago. She pulls out a pair of overalls. They are Gloria's. She
used to wear them all the time while she worked, trying to
channel the spirit of Janie from *Their Eyes Were Watching
God*. Or maybe just Minnie Riperton. Maria puts them to
her face and inhales and catches the scent of Dr. Hauschka.

By the time Gloria found out that the school was cutting
her funding and that she would have a month to move out
of graduate student housing, she'd become a real pack rat.
Over spring break, Maria flew home to help her move out.
She found Gloria surrounded by Afrocentric tchotchkes,

Native American beadwork, bottles upon bottles of Dr. Hauschka beauty products that she would never get around to using, boxes and boxes of rice pilaf and cans and cans of organic soup she would never get around to eating.

Gloria sat at the little table across from Maria sipping a cup of Lipton tea, saying she didn't know where she would go next. She actually thought maybe she could finish the dissertation in thirty days. The tome sat a foot high in her freezer, so that it wouldn't burn up in case of fire. Of course she had it on disks and such, but she still wanted a draft in that freezer. Maria stared at it when she went to get ice for her lemonade.

Gloria gazed off into space as she spoke. I should tell you—I'm having a little health hiccup.

What do you mean?

It's nothing. Just a thing Chuck noticed. A lump. Under my arm. He thinks he can treat it with remedies. We're going to try that first. My body is trying to tell me something. We're trying to figure out what it's trying to say.

Maria frowned at her mother. Maybe you should see a real doctor. It sounds serious.

Chuck is a real doctor. Well, he's more than that. He's a healer. I don't want to do anything that's going to make me sicker.

Gloria drove Maria to the airport the next evening. They sat inside the Legal Seafood in the terminal. There was something heavy hanging over them. Gloria looked thin, delicate. She didn't touch her chowder. She asked Maria questions about her classes but didn't seem entirely there. At the gate, she told Maria, Marry the narcoleptic shvartze with the fancy hair. He comes from good stock.

Back on campus, Maria found Khalil in his room in Ujamaa, fast asleep with Jimmy Cliff playing on the speakers and a copy of *Wired* magazine spread open on his lap. His dreadlocks reminded her of computer wires. She stared at his sleeping face. It really was remarkable, the way it held everything in it at once. She curled up beside him, hugging her own knees, feeling a wave of homesickness—a nameless dread.

She would never see Gloria well again.

There is a knocking on the bedroom door. She turns. It's Elsa.

We really should be getting to the circus, Maria. Did you pick out an outfit?

Maria drops Gloria's overalls onto the bed.

Elsa laughs when she sees them. Now remember, it's a circus, not a hayride.

I know. I was just—clearing out some old things.

Let me help you, okay?

Elsa goes to the closet and begins to rifle through her things. She pulls out a pair of dark jeans and a red blouse Maria bought for a job interview once upon a time.

This is totally perfect. Elegant but casual.

Maria puts on the outfit. Elsa says she wants to put a little makeup on Maria. Maria sits at the edge of the bed, her hands folded in her lap, her face tilted up, while Elsa works on her face. She fixes her eyes on Elsa's face, the spray of yellow curls and glassy blue eyes and toothy Scandinavian smile. She thinks about how lonely it must have been for Elsa growing up in the Era of Mulatto Martyrs. There aren't many of them in Elsa's age group, she's only met a few, they are a rare and flightless, near-extinct bird. Every time Maria meets one she is aware of her own dumb luck.

Are you doing okay, Maria? Elsa says, patting her face gently with a sponge dipped in foundation.

Maria doesn't want to go out today. She wants to stay home with Khalil. She is not so sure she wants to be in the movie anymore. She can't explain why. But she knows also that it is too late. They are all waiting for her out there. They have brought equipment. They have spent hours already filming them. It is too late to pull out.

It's just— Maria says.

Elsa is waiting. Just what?

It's just—they abuse animals in this circus, Maria says. I saw it on the news. They beat the elephants with steel poles.

Elsa laughs as if it were a joke. She blends the foundation into Maria's skin. Listen, she says, you look a little tired. Today is a cinch. You just have to walk around the edges of the tent holding hands with Khalil. Look surprised when you see Lisa. You don't have to say anything deep. It's footage. Filler. Just move your lips if you don't feel like actually talking. Recite the Pledge of Allegiance.

She steps back and cocks her head at Maria, sees something that needs fixing. Adds some more shadow to her eyes.

That's it. Lovely.

She squats down and holds Maria's hands, fixes her eyes on her. Maria feels like Elsa is her teacher and she is a child at a certain kind of school—one of those rich hippie schools where everyone seems so laid-back, but you end up feeling more ashamed.

I know you're nervous about the wedding. I can feel that. I mean, I've never been married myself, but it's normal to be anxious before such a big day. Such a big life change. But—well, can I tell you something?

Yeah.

I envy you a little bit. I mean, Khalil? Come on. He's a keeper. You couldn't dream up a more perfect guy.

Maria shifts a little, restless now. Well, okay.

Don't brush it off. Elsa's voice has a little more edge now. It's not something to shrug about. Not everyone gets so lucky. Not everyone gets to have the whole package. You and Khalil—you have a very important story to tell.

Right. Sure. Maria scratches a patch of eczema on her

hand and looks past Elsa at the door, eager now to actually be with Khalil.

Elsa smiles at her with all her Scandinavian teeth. Okay, let's move it. Lisa is meeting us soon. We can't have her waiting. You know how fierce Lisa can be when she's mad.

They both laugh and shake their heads. They have both been on the other end of Lisa's fire.

■　■　■

They walk the ten blocks to the circus.

Elsa explains along the way what her plan is. When they get to the circus, Maria and Khalil will "accidentally" bump into Lisa.

Act surprised when you see Lisa, okay? Elsa says.

You mean like this? Khalil says. Then in a high voice from the old Doug E. Fresh song: Oh, oh, oh my God!

Elsa laughs. Yeah, just like that. You are too funny, Khalil.

They arrive at the circus entrance. Maria is somehow surprised to see it is a real circus in the middle of Brooklyn. Outside the big tent are all the ingredients that make it a real circus: juggling clowns, a dunking booth, a mime in a tuxedo, a cage holding an anemic alligator.

Maria holds Khalil's hand as they meander through the crowd. Elsa and Ansel and Heather (whom everyone keeps calling Heidi) shadow them, filming. People in the crowd notice the camera crew, crane their necks, then fade to that dull look of disappointment when they see it's nobody famous.

Khalil does all the talking. He waves his hands around, while Maria smiles and nods and mutters encouragement. He's talking about his fledgling company, Brooklyn Renaissance. How he thinks it's going to blow up. How in five years it will go public. How they will be mad rich if that happens.

He slows his pace.

Hey, he says, squinting into the distance. What the—?

Maria laughs. You're a pretty good actor, she says. Is that your surprised look? I mean, if the computer mogul thing doesn't work out, you could be in movies for real.

He's points ahead. No, seriously. Look. It's Lisa—and she brought a man. Lisa got a man.

Maria sees through the crowd that it's true. There is Lisa in a head wrap. It is a bright Kenyan print today. The real shocker is that she's with a black man. Lisa with a black man. He is wearing a baseball cap pulled low over his eyes. Lisa is standing on tiptoe giving him a kiss. He's kissing her back. Maria can't see his face, but she can see enough to know he's no willowy white boy. She is amused. Maybe the times really are a-changin', she says. I mean, if an inveterate honky-lover like Lisa can go black.

Khalil ignores her. Sometimes he doesn't think she's funny. She's noticed this.

He calls out his sister's name. Lisa hears them and pulls away from the kiss and looks in their direction, waves. She wears a hapless, blushing grin.

Her man turns to look at them too, and at the sight of his face—for a brief moment—Maria is confused. She thinks he's a famous person. Lisa is kissing a famous person. She thinks he is an actor she has seen in a movie. Was it a Spike Lee movie?

But it's not an actor and he was never in a Spike Lee movie, and when she realizes her mistake, she stops in her tracks.

Wait, she says. Wait.

Everything is crazy. A little boy rushes past carrying a giant teddy bear, followed by an angry teenaged girl. Motherfucker, motherfucker, the girl is shouting at the boy. A clown on stilts teeters toward them wearing a rainbow Afro and a blue tuxedo, a red smile painted around the outline of his lips. Maria feels the earth tilting left, then right.

She does not understand. And then she does. Perfectly. How did she not see it earlier? How did she not know at the birthday dinner that it was heading in this direction? How did she not know that night at the bar that it was Lisa the poet was going to meet for dinner?

Khalil is looking back at her, his face tense.

What's wrong with you? he hisses. We're on camera. Keep walking.

He pulls her forward. Ansel's camera is pointed at her

face. She senses him zooming in on her and she fixes her expression into what she hopes is a smile.

Lisa is still waving at them.

The poet, beneath his baseball cap, wears a small sly smile. A faintly sadistic smile. Maria wonders if those are folds in the denim of his pants or if he has an erection from kissing Lisa.

Ansel is capturing everything on camera—Lisa hugging Maria before she can slide away. Lisa whispering in her ear, I was going to tell you about—this. Lisa glancing up at the poet and saying to him, You know Maria, right?

The poet's smile is false, uneasy. Yeah, we've met before.

He knows, Maria thinks. He knows. He has always known. He's a goddamned poet. Poets know.

Maria is about to join our family, Lisa says. She and Khalil are getting hitched in June. Did you know?

Yeah, the poet says. I saw it on the news.

Lisa laughs, swats his arm. Seriously though, she says, with unnecessary jubilance. I can't think of anybody I'd rather have for a sister.

She squeezes Maria's hand. Maria pulls hers away and sticks it in her pocket. Tonight she will wash it over and over again with dish detergent until her eczema patch is a weeping red thing.

Lisa has never been so nice to her before, never shown so much affection. She is brimming over with generosity because she's in love. She's got love to spare.

Khalil whispers to Maria, Say something. We're supposed to be talking. We're on film. Remember?

Maria recites in a flat voice: I pledge allegiance to the flag of the United States of America, and to the republic for which it stands, one nation under God, indivisible, with liberty and justice for all—

Are you okay? Lisa says.

I'm fine. Why wouldn't I be fine?

You look pale.

I am pale. Or did you forget that fact about me?

After she says it, she looks down, studies her shoes. She can't stand to look at Lisa. It's all fake. A fake frown, a fake arm squeeze, fake concern done for the benefit of the camera. Lisa is only pretending to care how Maria is doing. Beneath her frown, Maria can see that her face is aglow. She has the poet. She is in love. Maria feels the blood rushing to her forehead, smashing in waves against her skull. She thinks that the truth is Lisa doesn't care how anybody else is doing or what they are feeling. If Maria were to throw herself into the pit with the lions right now and get torn to bloody pieces, Lisa would have to pretend to be sad. Because she is in love. Nobody gives a damn about anybody else when they are in love.

Lisa and the poet are whispering to each other now, smiling into each other's eyes. Maria hears the words *semblance* and *hijinks* and she thinks maybe they are laughing at her. Elsa told them to pretend the cameras were not there, but now Maria turns and stares straight into the black circular eye of the lens and says, Stop, Ansel, please stop. Ansel keeps filming as if it hasn't heard her.

She says more loudly into the lens, I feel sick.

Elsa hears her this time. She steps forward.

Cut, cut. Looks like Maria's having a problem.

Elsa isn't baring those big teeth for once.

Khalil speaks to Elsa and Ansel and Heather in a whispered tone and Maria thinks he's explaining something about Maria. Apologizing for Maria having ruined all the fun. Maria wonders if she will be that kind of spouse—the one who makes it necessary for Khalil to whisper apologies as they rush home from gatherings. Will she be that spouse, that wife, who always ruins the dinner party?

Elsa nods and touches Khalil's arm, understanding. She says to her crew: Okay, Ansel, Heidi, Maria is feeling sick. We're going to need to wrap up. We can get something next weekend.

Heather seems to have given up on correcting everyone about her name. In a glum silence, she gathers the cables and loops them around her arm. Ansel looks like he wants to be somewhere very far away from this whole production, and Maria wonders if he's actually getting paid for his work. Khalil is slapping palms with the poet. Maria wonders where he learned to do that with his hands. She has never seen him so adept at the palm slapping.

Lisa steps toward Maria, her arms open, a worried look

on her face. She wants another hug, even though they hugged just minutes ago. Maria shrinks away from Lisa's open arms and says, I might be catching.

Lisa nods, pretends to look concerned again. The poet avoids Maria's eyes, mutters goodbye. He and Lisa move away, arm in arm, swallowed into the crowd. Elsa, her mouth fixed in an angry line, wanders off with the crew.

Maria is alone with Khalil. They walk back the way they came, through the neighborhood. Maria's bones feel tired, as if she is a much older woman. Arthritic. They pass a pizza joint. Moon faces stare out, chewing, from behind the glass. A little girl's voice somewhere out there says, That's disgusting, and her mother's voice says, It's rude to stare.

Earth to Maria. Earth to Maria.

Khalil is calling her.

What did you say?

I asked if you're going to be all right alone till Tuesday, Khalil says.

Alone? Why would I be alone?

Um, because I'm going away.

Where are you going?

Don't you listen to a word I say?

Khalil rarely gets angry at Maria, just like Elsa rarely stops smiling. But he sounds angry now. He says she needs to get her ears checked. He says she's known he was going away for weeks. He and Ethan are going away together for the next few days to meet with investors in San Francisco.

He won't return until Tuesday night. He's leaving this evening. They have discussed this more than once. Earth to Maria?

■ ■ ■

Back at the apartment, Khalil disappears into the bedroom, saying he has to pack for his trip. She paces around, chewing on her cuticles, trying not to think about what she saw at the circus. She can smell her own body odor. She can hear Khalil in the bedroom, zipping up a bag. He's whistling a tune; he always gets cheerful before trips.

She thinks sometimes that if she and Khalil had met a long time ago, when they were younger, they would never have been friends, and certainly would never have become lovers. While he was learning to code on his father's ancient Commodore 64, she was playing hours of Donkey Kong at her local arcade, snapping Bubble Yum with a group of ne'er-do-wells. While he was listening to the 2 Tones, she was listening to Mtume's Juicy Fruit. While he was reading *Mad* magazine, she was reading *Essence*. She thinks sometimes that had they met at any other moment than the Stanford Quad on that Thanksgiving Day, they would have looked past each other, through each other, as if they were each invisible.

Maria goes to the couch and pulls an afghan over her head. It is literally an afghan, a blanket Khalil's parents brought back from their travels to Afghanistan last summer. It still smells like another country. She sits beneath it for what feels like a long time, hugging her knees to her chest, trying to control her breathing.

There is still so much to uncover. Some days it feels like she will never be done with Jonestown. She will never get out alive. Just last week she learned about Hyacinth, a seventy-six-year-old black woman, born at the turn of the century, the daughter of a former slave. Hyacinth joined Jim Jones with her sister back in Indianapolis during the church's early days. She called him Father, sometimes Dad. She followed him out to California. She signed over her home to Jim Jones, signed over her social security checks and all her worldly possessions. She followed him to a foreign land, where she hoped to finally be free.

But from the time she arrived in Guyana, Hyacinth began to lose faith. Jonestown wasn't what she thought it would be. And on the last night, when he called everyone to the pavilion, she decided she was tired of his voice. She didn't believe in Jim Jones anymore. Her sister went to the meeting, but Hyacinth stayed in her room. And when she heard the armed guards moving around the compound in gangs, searching for stragglers to lead them to the pavilion, she lay down flat on the floor and scooted beneath her bed. The guards opened the door but did not see her there.

She waited for her sister and friends to come back from the meeting, but they stayed so late that eventually she fell asleep. When she woke up, it was Sunday morning. Jim Jones's voice was for once not booming over the loudspeakers. Hyacinth put on her glasses and rose and went outside to search for her sister. She said in her testimony that the sky that morning was so bright and clear. The storm of the day before had passed. The silence was unusual. She heard only parrots and macaws squawking. Even Mr. Muggs, the Jonestown mascot, that ever-grunting chimpanzee, had gone quiet. She made her way down the footbridge to the senior citizens' center where she usually got breakfast. It was there that she found the bodies.

Some were propped in sitting positions, covered in sheets, others lay flat on the ground on their faces. She moved around them until she found her sister. Hyacinth sat down beside her. For a while she thought maybe she herself was dead and this was the afterworld. And for a while she thought maybe the others were just sleeping.

For two days, Hyacinth wandered amongst the bodies. They were beginning to bloat and stink under the hot sun. Then one morning she heard the whir of a helicopter overhead and the voices of men on the ground.

In news reports later, the men—members of the Guyanese Defense Force—reported their shock at finding her there, an ancient woman, tiny and brown, blinking up at them from a sea of death.

Maria hears the car service beeping outside, Khalil rolling his bag into the hallway, the click of him opening the front door. She rises and heads outside in her socks, the afghan now draped over her shoulders. The air has the electric feeling of impending rain.

Khalil is already down the steps, putting his suitcase into the trunk of the black sedan. He looks handsome, dapper, in his camel-colored trench coat. He slams the trunk closed. Pauses. Watches her where she stands at the top of the steps.

What is it? he says. What's wrong?

Nothing, it's just— She touches her lips and shakes her head.

Khalil starts back up the steps toward her. You're crying, he says. I can cancel the trip if you want. Just say it. Ethan can do the meetings without me.

No, no. Go. I'm fine. I have work to do.

Okay, okay. But don't spend too much time alone. I mean, call Lisa if you need company.

She scoffs, looks away. I think Lisa's got other things on her mind.

Khalil wraps his arms around her.

She clings to him. He is a good man. A hard-to-find good man. Elsa is right. He is a keeper.

He tries to pull away but she won't let go. She can't let him go. It seems important that she not let him go.

Easy, tiger, he says, breaking out of her grip. I'm going to miss my flight.

He starts down the steps but glances back.

Your curls, he says. They're growing on me.

They both laugh at the way it sounds. And she thinks, laughing with him, just then, that they might pull it off. There is still time to pull it off, to shift the course of things inside her. She thinks back to the first time they spoke in the Quad that day. Remembers him on his skateboard, the sling on his arm, his Basquiat hair, the casual white boy smile cast into a brown boy's face. She took one look at him and knew he was the one. He is still that boy who inspired such clarity in her. She saw him and understood he was her fate. He is still the same boy. She is still the same girl. He waves at her, smiling behind the glass of the sedan, then the car pulls away.

Maria does not move to go inside. She thinks about surprises—how you can look at a thing for so long, can think you know it in its entirety, but there are always more surprises. When she began her research about Jonestown she thought she knew the story. She thought the only defectors were the ones who fled to an airstrip with the congressman. But she now knows there were a group of defectors who left in secret on that same morning. Eleven, all of them black, had been plotting their escape for months, whispering to one another that Another America felt more like the America they'd left behind, only worse; they'd noticed since arriving that the black people worked the fields and the top decision-makers were white. They didn't want to call Jim Jones Father. He was not their father.

On the morning the congressman left for the airstrip, they asked the guards if they could go on a picnic. Though they had no food and the sky was stormy, the guards said okay. They walked to the edge of the compound, then kept walking onward into the jungle.

They carried their babies strapped to their backs; they had drugged them with Flavor Aid mixed with Valium so they would not cry. They walked through the night and into the next morning. They walked for thirty hours straight, taking turns carrying the babies, not sure exactly where they were going or what they'd left behind.

It has begun to rain, softly. Maria has the sense of being watched. Across the street, she glimpses a figure standing in a third-story window, watching her. The figure is small and gray with a pale face and it stands behind a gauzy curtain. At first glance it looks like a child, but no, she thinks it is somebody older, much older. She thinks it is the old Creole woman, the one who dresses all in white. She lifts her hand to wave. But the figure doesn't move or wave back and Maria understands it is not a person after all.

Inside, she turns on the television. *Seinfeld* is on. The sound of the actors' voices reminds her of Khalil. She goes to the bookshelf by the window. There is a framed photograph of her and Khalil on graduation day. They each wear a cap and gown and each also wear a kente cloth sash over their shoulders. They bought the sashes a week before graduation from a kiosk in the campus plaza where a white man had materialized one day, balding and pink, to sell various theme sashes for graduation day. He sold graduation sashes for every identity: Greek sashes, ethnic sashes, gay sashes. The day before graduation he disappeared, like Mr. Monkey McBean with his Star-Off machine.

Most of the black students bought the kente cloth sashes and wore them, save for a few miscellaneous types. The sashes were proof that they were still black even after four years at the Farm. No matter how much money they would make someday, no matter how many white people they would fuck or marry, no matter how light-skinned their children, no matter how many times they listened to Joni Mitchell in the years that would come, the sashes were there to tell them and anyone who was looking their way that they had not lost their negritude out there in the Rodin sculpture garden.

In the photo Maria and Khalil appear so young, like puppy versions of their current selves, the subcutaneous fat still plump beneath their skin. They are laughing, arms around each other, in the Quad, wearing those goddamned corny kente cloth sashes.

Maria can see Lisa standing off to the side, at a distance, in a red dress and low heels. The expression she wears in the photo isn't really a smile. It is more like a sneer. She looks like any other angry second child, sulking and acne pocked, watching her golden brother have his day of glory.

She's not as pretty in the picture from the past as she is

now. She has never been as pretty as she is now. She just keeps getting better looking. By the time she is dead, Maria thinks, she will be stunning.

Maria puts the photo back on the shelf facing backward, so that she and Khalil and Lisa are staring at the wall.

The *Seinfeld* theme song is playing—the pluck of guitar strings signifying the end of another episode, or maybe the beginning of the next. George's face is no longer blue. Yes, now another episode is coming. It's a *Seinfeld* marathon. A new *Seinfeld* is always beginning. She's seen this one before. It's the episode where Jerry can't remember the name of his girlfriend. Khalil likes *Seinfeld*. So does Ethan. Sometimes he comes over just to sit watching it with Khalil

Ethan once, about a year ago, described the characters in *Seinfeld* as New York intellectuals. That's how he said it.

Maria was in the room with them at the time and she asked Ethan what made the characters intellectual. Was it just the fact that they were white? Because as far as she could see they were anything but intellectual.

After she said it Ethan stared at her with such loathing she was certain he was going to strike her, but again, he didn't. Khalil made a joke about all of them being children of academics, and, like magic, Ethan became merry and harmless again.

It is dark outside of the window. The clock reads seven. Khalil is already on the plane, barreling west across the sky with Ethan at his side.

She is hungry. Hungrier than she has ever been in her life. She needs to get food. Meat. She must be iron-deficient. She has to have meat.

She will just run out quickly and get some chicken or ribs. She will be back shortly to finish watching the episode. She wants to find out what happens, if Jerry ever figures out his girlfriend's name. She heads out, leaving the lights and the television on. She will be that quick.

It is no longer raining. The street glimmers beneath the street lamp. The pavement is still wet, the air has that post-rain clarity. She walks to the place where they sell Jamaican jerk chicken and goes inside and stands in line and orders a plate of food. She sits at a small linoleum table and hunches over the plate and eats the chicken with her fingers until it is just a pile of bones on her plate. Sated, she wipes her mouth with her sleeve and takes a gulp from the fruit drink that came free with her meal. It is not the food she usually eats but it is delicious.

Afterward, Maria stands outside the chicken joint for a while, just breathing in the cool night air. She knows she should go home. It is time to go home. She left the television on. She left the apartment waiting for her to return. And yet, almost like somebody in a trance, when she leaves the restaurant she turns left instead of right. She walks to the train station and swipes her card through the turnstile and heads underground and waits at the platform, watching rats scurry around the tracks. The train isn't crowded yet. The night is young. She finds a seat between two old people. She thinks how Khalil is high in the sky and she is beneath the earth. She thinks about their registry. Wonders how much of the shit they put on the list they will actually receive. She thinks about Jim Jones. She thinks about how so many of the people who died there were black. How many of them were old. It was like a giant black nursing home. And how much Jim Jones loved black people before he killed them. What a warrior against racism.

He even insisted on calling them white nights, those occasions when he'd call them into the pavilion under duress. He didn't want to use the word *black* to signify terror, emergency. Jones felt there was too much negativity already assigned to the idea of blackness.

So those nights of terror he called white nights, when he would rouse the sleeping people under cloak of darkness, summon them over the loudspeakers to the pavilion, crying out, Alert! Alert!

Obedient, the people would rise from their beds in their pajamas and walk through the darkness to the center of the compound where he waited. There, they would stand before him, the white man they called Father, and listen to him rant. Each time he told them the same story: The American government was moving in for an attack. It was imminent. Couldn't they hear the forces coming?

Indeed, they heard voices, sounds of machetes hacking through the jungle. How could they not believe him? They had each left for a reason. They knew their government was capable of great evil.

Father himself was weeping, half-mad with grief. What to do, where to go? He said it was an emergency. Couldn't they hear the planes in the distance? They were coming to bomb them, to spray them with poisonous gas. He rattled off their options: They could go to the Soviet Union. They could fight back against their attackers. Or they could choose revolutionary suicide. Father voted for suicide.

Mothers, he said, don't let them take your babies. They will torture your babies.

To me death is not a fearful thing, he said. It's the living that is treacherous.

On those white nights, the people drank what he gave them without protest. They squirted the purple liquid down the throats of their babies. Afterward, they stood in the dark, weeping, clutching one another, as they waited for death to take them. But it didn't. Five minutes, ten minutes, twenty minutes, an hour later, nothing happened. And with the sunlight rising over Guyana, Jones would tell them it was only a test. The Flavor Aid was just Flavor Aid. He was only testing them. You're still alive, he'd say. Isn't that beautiful? It was only a test.

The subway rises out of the station, rumbles across the bridge toward the mass of Manhattan. She thinks about the television set back at the apartment, how the laugh track of *Seinfeld* is filling the empty room.

oward the end of her days, when Gloria was in hospice, she seemed to split into three people. The nurses at the hospice called it "sundowning," something where dying people grow confused at the end of each day, when the light shifts. But really, it seemed like something else to Maria. It seemed she had split into three distinct personalities. Like Sybil, she even spoke with distinct voices and referred to herself by three different names, depending on the evening.

Some nights she was Beth Ann. That was what she called herself. Beth Ann was all gravelly, kindhearted wisdom. She believed in homeopathy and hugs and medicinal mushrooms. The nurses in the hospice liked Beth Ann. She spoke in uplifting, quasi-Buddhist aphorisms. Not all paths are straight and not all meanings are apparent! Enjoy your journey! Everything Beth Ann said had an exclamation point at the end.

Other nights, she became Nigel, a haughty British anthropologist who liked to ramble on about all he'd learned on his extensive world travels. Nigel was an unapologetic lech. He spoke to women—the nurses, female visitors—with his eyes fixed boldly on their breasts.

Nigel once told Maria that women were like fruit: Different races of women, he said, ripen at different ages, and you had to know this before you plucked one. He kept calling Maria "son." He told Maria that WASP women ripened too early—at puberty—and their beauty faded and withered each year that followed. He said Jewish girls ripened at about thirty, just in time for childbearing, when their hair grew thick and shiny, their zaftig breasts ready to spout milk. He said black women ripened slowly, like wine, and came to fruition in middle age. Son, Nigel said, that's why a black woman is a good investment; she's sweetest when she's fifty.

Other nights, Gloria was just Gloria, but those were the worst of all because she didn't recognize Maria. She would give Maria the side eye, as if she were a stranger.

When the nurses came to check Gloria's vitals, she would pull them close and whisper to them, loud enough so that Maria could hear, This strange girl keeps showing up. Can you tell me where she comes from? She's actually starting to give me the creeps.

T he fire station is alive with activity. Maria stands on the sidewalk, watching through the open garage door. The firemen inside must have just returned from putting out a fire. Their faces are streaked with ash. They are changing out of their uniforms. They stand half in and half out of their suits, their bare chests rippling, taut. They look like Chippendales dancers, secretarial porn. Maria feels a predictable tremor of desire at the sight of these half-nude white men, but it is more like a memory of desire than the real thing.

Once upon a time she would have wanted a man like

this. A hero out of a history book—someone who would pull her from a burning fire. Khalil showed up instead. It was Khalil who took her hand and led her to safety.

She takes one final glance at the firemen, then heads down the avenue, turns one corner, then another, until she is there, on the poet's street. She looks up at the windows. There is a light on in one of them. If she blurs her eyes right it looks like a fire burning.

She digs around in her purse. She still has the extra set of keys she stole from Susan's apartment. They have been lurking in the bottom of this bag for months. She lets herself inside. The stairwell smells of bleach and pizza. She climbs upward, wearily, doggedly, on legs that feel much older than twenty-seven years.

It seems like a lifetime since she began her dissertation. She knew then only the barest of facts about the Peoples Temple Agricultural Project. She now knows so much more.

On the recording Jones made of the day they all died, there seems to be music playing like a dirge under the cheers and screams of the people. For so long Maria was not able to identify the song they were playing. Now she knows there is nothing there. The music on that final audio, the tape the FBI calls Q042, was always just a shadow. The backward lyrics, the slowed-down organ, are echoes from a previous recording. On the day they all died, they was no music playing.

The people still believed, until the weary end, that the man they called Father had their best interest in mind. They were old and they were black. They were young and they were white. They were children and they were parents.

Jim Jones said, Take this poison and drink from this cup. This is the blood of Christ. Drink from it and you will be free.

A woman named Christine Miller—a sixty-year-old black woman, a longtime member of the church—was one in a thousand voices. She was not in a trance. On the death tape, she is the sole voice who steps up to the microphone and pleads with Jim Jones to reconsider. She is the sole voice to disagree with his plan to kill them all. She asks if Russia is still an option. Or Cuba. He tells her it is too late for Russia, and Cuba. But I look at all the babies, Christine Miller says, and I think they deserve to live.

Jones says the babies deserve peace. Without me, he says, life has no meaning. I'm the best friend you'll ever have. Revolutionary suicide is the only way to go. The decision has been made. All hope is lost. Christine Miller's voice is drowned out by the rage of the collective. In the background are the sounds of screams, children crying, mothers weeping. A rising hysteria. Jones, like a scolding parent, orders them to die with dignity. Are we not black, proud, and socialist?

The last thing that can be heard on the tape is Jones

shouting out over the loudspeaker—Mother, mother, mother, mother, mother!—followed by silence.

■ ■ ■

The hallway floor looks dimmer, narrower than she remembered. The other apartments are silent. She presses her ear to his door. It seems to pulse beneath her skin. She can hear music playing within. The tune is familiar, a song she loved once. Luther Vandross. *Long ago, and oh so far away*, he sings with silky wonder. She used to listen to Luther in her pantry bedroom, trembling with sadness and longing for some delicate boy she'd never met.

Maria knows that Luther Vandross usually means one thing. The poet is not alone. But she tries to keep hope alive. Maybe he is alone. Maybe he's in there waiting for Maria to come to him. He's already dumped Lisa. He dumped her at the UniverSoul circus just this afternoon, surrounded by clowns and jugglers. Maybe Lisa was always just a pawn in his plan to get closer to Maria. Maybe his goal from the start was to marry into the same family as Maria so they could remain linked in an illicit love affair. A desperate, foolish move, yes, but maybe.

Maria tries his door. It's locked of course. She expected this. She goes next door and tries the key she still has in Susan's door, and it works. How odd, Maria thinks, as she steps inside, that after everything that happened, it did not occur to Susan to change the lock.

Susan's apartment smells of the baby. Everyone is sleeping. There are only night sounds—a humming refrigerator, the ticking of a clock. Maria moves softly, stealthily, into the living room. The television is on, but the sound is off. It's an infomercial for a ThighMaster. It flickers onto the sofa, illuminating a woman who lies prone, fully dressed, asleep in its glare. There is a bag of potato chips and a half-empty bottle of Beaujolais open on the coffee table before her.

The woman is not Susan. She has dark hair and skin the same shade as Maria's. It must be Consuela. The real Consuela, like the Real Roxanne. Maria edges closer to get a better look. She is startled to see a much older woman, heavy-set and middle-aged, with gray streaks in her hair. She is a woman of a certain age, with coarse plain features, pockmarked skin. Maria tries to remember what she herself looks like, but she draws a blank. Her eyes sting as she backs away from the sleeping woman, and she turns away and heads toward the bedroom. It's a mess. The bed is piled with clothes and baby paraphernalia. Maria glances in at June. She's asleep in the squalor, on her back, her face tilted up to the ceiling. Maria can see she's grown since the last time she saw her. Susan has at least been feeding her.

Maria doesn't dawdle. She has to get to the poet. She starts toward the window, but midway there she steps on something and laughter fills the room. It's a Monchhichi doll. She has somehow stepped on a talking Monchhichi doll. The laughter dies out after some seconds, but it's too late. June is awake. She begins to whimper.

Maria stands frozen, waiting for the baby to fall back asleep. She has to fall back asleep. But the whimper is turning into a cry.

Maria leans over the crib, trying to shush her with a finger to her lips, but at the sight of Maria's face June begins to cry harder, a bleating, angry sound.

Come on, Maria whispers. Come on, mi hija. She says it with a Spanish accent. She picks up a nubby pink blanket and tries to lay it over the baby, thinking it might comfort or warm her, but she fights it off.

Sighing, Maria picks up the baby. She lifts her up and down, swings her around in a circle. She attempts a smile. She sings. *Welcome, welcome all of you, we're so glad you are here with us.* It's that song from the album, the children's cut, the one she has been listening to for years. She pretends they are having fun. But the baby only screams louder. It is the sound of the biggest mosquito in the world. Maria swings June around in a faster, wider circle, her hands gripping beneath the baby's armpits, so that the legs dangle free. The baby looks shocked by the motion, but only stops screaming to take bigger gulps of air and start her shrill siren wail all over again.

She picks up the rubber giraffe that lies nearby. She tries

to put it in June's mouth, remembering from last time that the baby liked to suck on it, but June bats it away and screams louder. Hers is a war cry. She must have learned it at that Beijing orphanage. The survivors cry the loudest. Maria taps the giraffe against June's lips, saying, Take it, come on. Just take it. June turns her head from side to side, sneering, squawking, as if offended by the peace offering. Nothing is good enough for this baby. Maria feels the tightening sensation in her brain. She shakes the baby, jostles her, whispering to her she needs to be quiet. She just wants to surprise her out of her fury, the way men in old movies slap the hysterical woman across the face. She thinks if she can just startle June she will calm down and understand that she's acting crazy, that it's not an emergency. She will know that Maria was just passing through the bedroom, not even planning to hang out. She shakes her, saying, calm down, just calm the fuck down.

The baby does go quiet then. Maria holds her in the stillness, feeling the warmth and weight of her body in her arms, smelling her own pungent odor rise up around them.

On the last night at the hospice, Gloria returned to herself. Her other personas, the aging anthropologist, the New Age sass, dissipated, and she was Gloria again. She seemed to recognize Maria too, though it wasn't entirely clear. She lifted a bony arm and pointed weakly at her where she sat at the bedside and said Oh, oh, it's you. She patted the edge of her bed and Maria climbed into her mother's bed and lay beside her under the sheets. Gloria was so tiny in her last hours. Nobody had ever told Maria how people disappear in stages. Every moment Gloria seemed to grow smaller. In her delirium, she kept calling Maria 'Mama,' and crying to her about some fig tree she'd fallen out of as a child. She kept asking, Where did you go? Where did you go all this time? Maria held Gloria like a baby and stroked her brow and said, There, there. She patted Gloria's back as if she were her real mother, telling her lies like a real mother. Everything's going to be all right. It's going to be fine. There's nothing to be afraid of.

The night was long and full of false stops and machines beeping in the dark and at some point Maria fell into a dreamless sleep. She woke to find Gloria stiff and cold beside her, her eyes wide open like she'd been startled. The nurses came to tend to the body and told Maria she was free to go. On her way out of the hospice, they gave her a clear plastic bag holding Gloria's belongings. Her Birkenstocks inside looked like giant dog chews.

Maria senses a presence. The gray thing. She is not alone. There is somebody here with her. But when she turns around she sees it is not the gray thing at all. It is Consuela. She has risen finally from her Beaujolais slumber and is watching Maria from the doorway, her eyes large, fingers held over her lips. She asks a question in Spanish, then some fog falls away and she rushes toward Maria and yanks the baby out of her arms. She backs away, stroking June's hair, half crying, and disappears into the other room. Maria can hear her picking up the phone, punching in numbers.

Maria goes to the window and climbs out onto the fire escape, the way she did before. She pulls the window shut behind her. The night air feels cold against her skin. She stands panting for a moment, searching the sky for a pinprick of light. An airplane moving west. She sees nothing, just darkness in all directions.

Distantly, she hears a siren. She crouches low and crawls along the metal landing until she is outside of the poet's window. It is open a crack and she pulls it up and climbs inside, sliding the window closed behind her.

Luther Vandross is no longer playing. There is no music. She can hear a shower running. The apartment looks somehow duller, more ordinary than it did the first time. She sees a girl's ankle boots lying on the floor beside the sofa, a purse open there. She goes to the purse and opens it. She takes out the wallet, looks inside, though she already knows whose face she will see on the photo ID. She stares at the face behind the plastic. It's not a good picture. Lisa's hair has been hot-combed to straightness. She looks ordinary, sullen, plain without the curls, without the objet d'art head wrap. She doesn't look anything like the doll Khalil and Maria had made in her image, the doll by Ceres Dalton.

She puts the wallet away and heads toward the sound of the shower. The bathroom door is open a crack. Maria peeks inside. The air is so steamy; she can just make out human shapes behind the frosted pebbled glass. She hears their laughter and whispers beneath the steady stream of water. They don't see her. They don't sense her. She wonders what would happen if she went inside and stepped up to the glass and pressed her face against it. At what point would they notice her there?

Out in the building's corridor there are sounds of a commotion. Official footsteps, a police radio, a woman speaking in Spanish. Then a sudden and stern knocking on the poet's door.

Maria turns and ducks into the poet's bedroom. There is a space between his dresser and his desk. She slips inside the space and crouches there, hugging her knees. She can hear everything from here. The shower turning off. The glass door sliding open. Their voices. His and Lisa's.

Are you expecting somebody?

No. Wait here.

The poet's footsteps crossing the apartment, the front door opening, his voice speaking in low tones to the police. Consuela is out in the hallway too. Maria can hear her saying something about a bruja. That's the word she uses. *Bruja.* Other neighbors have come out into the hall to see what is the matter. Bewildered questions fly. Beneath it all, Maria can make out another sound, a familiar gnat-like buzz. Baby June. Hers is a survivor orphan's warrior cry.

The poet raises his voice, trying to be heard over the wailing: No, officer, nobody came around here.

The sound of the baby awakes something inside of her. She must think. She must act. She crawls on all fours toward the poet's bed and scoots underneath. It is a shallow space. She is still holding the rubber giraffe in her hand. She can hear Lisa out there. She has somehow emerged from the bathroom, dewy and clean, to join the conversation at the front door. Maria imagines her wearing the poet's bathrobe, the head wrap discarded, her curls dripping wet around her face.

The conversation in the other room goes on for a long time. Until finally it is over. She hears the door click shut. She hears their voices in the kitchen. They are having a midnight snack together. A refrigerator door opening and closing. Their voices speaking in low serious tones. Pouring drinks. Clinking glasses. A sound of chairs scraping the floor.

They return to the bedroom. Maria holds her breath. She can see their bare feet beside the bed—his long and flat, hers smaller, with a high arch, the toenails painted burgundy. They are kissing. She hears the sucking noises. They fall on top of the mattress, which sinks lower over Maria's face. They roll around, slurping each other. Maria has to turn her face to the side to avoid her nose getting bruised in the sexual games that follow. It is disgusting to her what they do. Wholesome. It is not the best sex she's ever heard, but it's not the worst either. It's real sex with real people. There is tender sighing and rhythmic grunting. She bites on the giraffe to keep from screaming. Her mouth fills with the taste of rubber.

She thinks about the men who were the first to arrive by helicopter. They said it was unclear what they were looking at from up above. They said it looked like the world's largest patchwork quilt spread out on the ground. They said it looked like a giant used car lot—all those specks of bright color. So many different colors. It was only when they got down to three hundred feet that the smell hit them. Unmistakable.

Above Maria's head, the sex is over. They are talking. Pillow talk.

Do you think someone really tried to steal that baby?

I doubt it. The nanny probably made the whole thing up.

Why would she lie?

Maybe she was losing her shit. I wouldn't blame her. I had to listen to that baby cry day and night. I mean, I've almost called the cops on that baby a few times myself.

You're bad.

Roll over. Let me spoon you.

The mattress shifts, sinks lower so it is touching Maria's nose.

Hey, he says.

Yeah?

You're real cool people. I'm—I'm glad you're here. You know?

More wetness. Sucking. Finally, silence. Their breathing deepens into sleep.

From beneath, Maria can see the poet's desk, his computer, a stack of books, manuscript pages. She can see their clothes strewn on the floor, pants legs entangled. She can see the dusky light, half blue, half gray. It is the hour between—still dark enough that she can crawl away. She can still go back. But she is so tired. Her bones feel heavy, ancient, like those of a much older woman. She closes her eyes, thinking she will just rest for a moment, and drifts off into another time and space. In the dream, she is there with all the people. They are watching the sky for the airplane that will take them home. In the dream, there is still time. But when she opens her eyes, she sees it is too late. The night has passed. A white light fills the room.